CANDY HARPER

HAVE a little FAITH

SIMON AND SCHUSTER

First published in Great Britain in 2013 by Simon and Schuster UK Ltd
A CBS COMPANY

Copyright © 2013 Candy Harper

1 3 5 7 9 10 8 6 4 2

Simon & Schuster UK Ltd
1st Floor
222 Gray's Inn Road
London WC1X 8HB

Simon & Schuster Australia, Sydney
Simon & Schuster India, New Delhi

A CIP catalogue record for this book is available
from the British Library.

PB ISBN: 978-0-85707-823-0
EBook ISBN: 978-0-85707-824-7

Printed and bound by CPI Group (UK) Ltd, Croydon, CR0 4YY

www.simonandschuster.co.uk
www.simonandschuster.com.au

For Susan.
Thank you for all the laughs we have had
and the ones we've got to come.

SEPTEMBER

MONDAY 5TH SEPTEMBER

That's it. I am never going to school again.

I was woken up this morning by Dad doing some brutal curtain opening and entirely unnecessary breathing and existing. He said, 'Wake up, sweetheart. First day back at school!'

Urgh. He only calls me 'sweetheart' when he wants me to do some hideous job like laying the table or kissing Granny. Then he started his New Term Lecture.

'Let's put last term behind us. I want you to really do your best for me, Faith. That's all I'm going to say. That and be good.' He tried to look stern. 'Be *really good* because you wouldn't like the uniform at military school.'

Please. My elderly relatives (AKA: Mum and Dad) have made such a fuss about me treating Year Ten as a 'fresh start' that you would think that my school career so far had consisted of maiming and mentally scarring teachers on a daily basis.

Whereas, we all know it was just that one time.

Despite all this nonsense, I was actually looking forward to going to school this morning. I even made the effort to straighten my hair *and* open my eyes *and* get out of bed (not in that order because the last time I tried that there was some sheet scorching and Dad warned me that the fire station are getting fed up of him ringing them 'every five minutes').

So, there I was, arriving in my tutor room on the dot of 9.07 (ish), quite prepared to do my best at ignoring Mrs Hatfield dribbling on, so Megs and I could have a good chat about important things like finding some actual male-type boys to spend time with this term, when our head of year, Miss Ramsbottom, appeared and glared at me. Miss Ramsbottom is about nine-foot tall with shiny black hair and very pale skin. She looks like a supermodel who died and was brought back to life by vampires. Her eyes are always rimmed in eyeliner and it is quite hard to ignore her glaring at you, so once I'd finished explaining to Megs how to apply blusher to create the illusion of cheekbones, I was forced to give Miss Ramsbottom my attention. Miss Ramsbottom does not like me and she was clearly enjoying herself while she told us some truly tragic news.

Megs and I are being split up!

It is outrageous. Megs has been my best friend ever since Year Seven; I don't think I could cope without her to carry out all the most special duties of friendship like feeding me sweeties when my hands are busy texting and checking my hair looks good from the back. But Miss Ramsbottom doesn't care about any of that. She is moving me to a different tutor group with no thought to how I will live without my best friend. Now who will give me piggybacks when I'm tired or tell me when I've got one of those dangly bogies?

What, you may ask, could we possibly have done to deserve such despicable treatment? I asked the same question, in a polite yet assertive fashion, 'Why, Miss? *Why? Oh why? Oh why?*'

The evil Miss Ramsbottom did some wittering and blithering and nonsense-talking about some 'incidents' last term. When are they going to let that go? A few hilarious limericks posted on the school website, one teacher with a radical new haircut (which was an improvement anyway) and a minor explosion. You'd think they'd be pleased that we're so lively and innovative, but no, they have torn me away from my best mate. I am devastated.

In the afternoon we had an assembly with our ancient headmistress Miss Peters. Miss Pee is one of those older ladies who pretend to be nice by wearing pastel colours and taking an interest in the Special Needs group's poems about autumn, but behind closed doors I reckon she would tear off her own mother's head if it improved the exam grades of the school. The woman is pure steel.

At the start of assembly Miss Pee silenced us all with her death-laser stare and patted her helmet-like grey perm to make sure that no hair had dared struggle its way out of eight layers of hairspray, then she started banging on about how our rubbish school provides opportunities for us to blossom. How can I blossom without Megs? They shouldn't be allowed to inflict such torture on me. To make them pay I have decided I will not be returning to school.

Now all that's left to do is to tell Mum and Dad.

Might just eat a HobNob (or six) to keep my sugar levels up during my announcement.

LATER
They don't seem that keen.

LATER STILL
In fact, Dad threatened to cut off my allowance and several of my limbs if I don't go to school tomorrow. I thought that my hippy-pants mum might be supportive of me educating myself, but she was on Dad's side.

I said, 'I thought you believed that life is an education and that the landscape around us is nature's great university. Don't you think that a child should be educated in a home environment?'

Mum sniffed. 'I do, but only if the child isn't likely to burn the home environment down if she's left alone in it.' Which is a very unfair reference to a little accident I had when I tried to create a romantic atmosphere for my parents' anniversary by lighting a few candles.

I started losing my cool at that point and Mum said perhaps I should try some meditation to calm down (I'd rather have my arms chopped off) then Sam, my little brother from hell, said, 'Dad, perhaps you should think about it. If Faith can't cope at Westfield High, maybe you should send her to one of those special schools where they have people to help you to go to the toilet.' Then he started whining that his arm was broken, which is nonsense because I didn't hear it crack when I was twisting it.

LATEREST
I've been sent to my room.

This is all that Ramsbottom woman's fault. Why does she hate me so much? Obviously I hate her right back, but she started it. Actually, on my very first day in Year Seven when I saw Miss Ramsbottom I thought she looked kind of cool with her nice haircut and her super-high heels, but that afternoon she made me look like an idiot and I have never forgiven her. It happened in one of her ridiculous assemblies where she thinks what she is saying about not walking on the grass or remembering to curtsey when we see her is so important that we must use every fibre of our being to listen and therefore not breathe, blink, discuss last night's TV, or any other vital thing.

In the morning we'd had PE; the teacher, Miss Williams (AKA: Killer Bill), had enjoyed torturing us so much that we finished late, which meant we barely had time to get changed before we were whizzed off to assembly. I was already busting for the loo, but I didn't dare wander off because I wasn't sure if I could find the assembly by myself. So I filed into the hall and sat on a bench with my legs crossed while Ramsbottom launched into a list of thirty-seven things we must always remember to do, followed by a list of seventy-two things we must never do. I wasn't sure how much longer I could hold on. I couldn't just slip out either because I didn't know where the loos were. (You'd think that they'd point that sort of thing out on a school tour, wouldn't you? Much more helpful than where the library is, who needs to know that?) I tried to be sensible and mature about my predicament – which didn't come easily – by discreetly sidling up to my new form tutor, Mrs Hatfield, and asking if I could go to the loo. But Miss Ramsbottom is so insecure in herself that she couldn't compete with even a tiny bit of whispering in the corner. She stopped in the middle of what she was saying about fire alarms and stared at me, which meant everyone in the hall turned around and stared at me too. Then she said, 'I'll wait for you to finish because obviously the safety of the entire year is not as important as your full bladder.'

By this point, I was actually having to wiggle a little bit to stop myself from peeing, so it was pretty obvious that I did need the loo, and everybody laughed. Fortunately, my form tutor wasn't a total witch so she pulled me out of the hall and pointed me in the direction of the toilets. But for a long time my nickname was Full Bladder Faith.

No wonder I hate Miss Ramsbottom. I just don't know why she would hate such a delightful person as myself.

TUESDAY 6TH SEPTEMBER

It's awful being away from Megs. I'm sure Miss Ramsbottom looked particularly smug today because she knows I'm suffering. She obviously thinks that she is superior to us just because she is tall and has manicured nails and really expensive shoes. (What use are they to her? She must be at least thirty, she'll be dead soon, she should give them to someone who still has time to enjoy them.)

But, even though she has thrown us into different tutor groups to keep us apart, Ramsbottom seems to have forgotten that Megs and I are both geniuses. (Actually she did once call us geniuses, but she put the word 'evil' in front so I don't think she meant it as a compliment.) Anyway, because we are both so smart I still get to see Megs in top-set English, Maths and Science, which I suppose is better than nothing.

The one good thing about my new tutor group is that my friend from primary school, Lily, is in it. I love Lily, I really do, but she is a bit what the teachers call 'special' and everyone else calls utterly bonkers. I like hanging out with Lily, but she's not Megs.

I thought Lily was odd, but then I spent some time with the rest of my new class. They really are weird. Mostly, it seems that 10SW like hanging around talking about what the teachers are wearing and what answers they got for last night's Geography homework.

Like I said, weird.

LATER

When I got home I rang Megs.

'Megs, do you realise that we have spent a mere two hundred and seven minutes chatting today?' I said.

'I'm not surprised. It's all part of a pattern. You never bring me flowers any more. You don't notice when I get my hair cut. Sometimes I wonder if you ever really loved me. I try to reach out to you, but it's like you're on another planet.'

'I am. I am on planet 10SW. Do you know that for charity week they want to do a knit-a-thon?'

'I hate Miss Ramsbottom.'

'It makes me happy to think that the universe must hate her too. After all she is called Rams*bottom*.'

'You're right. It is quite helpful when people are named in a way that tells you what they're like. They should do the same thing with boys.'

'Megs, it would get very confusing if *all* boys were called Thicky McSmelly.'

WEDNESDAY 7TH SEPTEMBER

I was almost in tears at the breakfast table this morning. I said, 'Please try to understand, Mum: being without Megs is making me very sad. I also think that it may be affecting my academic performance.'

'Why's that?'

'I've got French this morning and I really can't do French without Megs.'

Sam interrupted with a mouth full of Chocolate Crispies. 'You're always saying how brilliant you are at French.'

'I am. But the only person who understands the French I speak is Megs. Madame Badeau speaks the old-fashioned kind where you're not allowed to use any English words.'

Mum just tutted and told me that I needed to 'think globally' and that I should be a friend to the world, not just to Megs. I asked her when was the last time the world lent me its lip-gloss? But she wasn't listening, so I moped my way to school.

When I got there Megs started nagging me about signing up for choir. 'The list's up on the notice board. You've got to join with me,' she said, in what she thinks is a sugary voice, but sounds more like when you sick-up Ribena and it burns your throat.

I said, 'I don't want to join your yickety choir. It's not cool, or fun or an acceptable use of my time. I don't like Mr Millet, and his music room smells like pee. Actually, I am going to go out on a limb here and suggest that it is, in fact, Mr Millet's own pee that is stinking the room out. I think when he goes to the loo he waves his thingy about like a conductor's baton and the pee gets all over his shoes. Besides, I lost all interest in music in Year Three when they tried to get me to play a recorder and I realised that Gavin Hitchins had already half filled it with dribble.'

'There's going to be a joint Christmas concert with Radcliffe boys' school, so lots of them will be coming here to rehearse with us once a week.'

I was unable to reply because I was sprinting

for the notice board and I find I can't mix exercise and speech.

When I'd made sure that my name was definitely on the list in big black letters I said to Megs, 'I can't believe the Radcliffe boys are coming here. Usually the St Mildred's girls hog them for themselves.'

St Mildred's is the girls' school on the other side of town. The girls there think they're better than us just because they're all filthy rich and super good-looking. In the last couple of years St Mildred's have managed to wangle doing a musical, a sponsored walk and a science fair with the Radcliffe boys. It's about time those harpies let us have a chance. I can hardly wait to get my first look at the boys. I hope they are all really fit and not just a bunch of boy-band wannabes.

I don't know why I ever disliked school. Of course, there is that business of the early mornings, the crushing of my soul and the mindless waste of the best years of my life, but you have to hand it to them. Rounding up a herd of boys and arranging them around a piano for my enjoyment is quite a nice way to say, 'Sorry about all that'. Isn't it?

THURSDAY 8TH SEPTEMBER

This morning I convinced Lily that what we needed to brighten our bleak morning were a couple of comedy moustaches. Unfortunately, I couldn't find the emergency ones that I normally take to school (I reckon Sam's been in my bag again) so I had to improvise with an eyeliner. I had a bit of a walrussy one and Lily had a little toothbrush one. We looked pretty dashing, if I say so myself, and even though 10SW are a bit boring, they seemed quite perked up by the change. Lily's tiny friend, Angharad, laughed so hard that she blew a snot bubble.

My new tutor, Mrs Webber, came in and did the register without saying a word. Then she read out some exciting notices about Xylophone Club and the Country Dancing team. Everyone was nudging each other waiting for Mrs W to notice our new look.

I put my hand up and said, 'I was wondering if we would be having one of those special chats from the nurse this term. You know, where we get to talk about our developing bodies and that. I've got some questions about unwanted facial hair.'

There was an explosion of sniggering.

Mrs Webber said, 'When the nurse does come in, perhaps I'll ask her if there's a particularly painful injection available to cure interminable teenage cheekiness.'

Then she got on with handing out academic target sheets for us to fill in. Smooth.

As we were going out the door she said, 'Faith.'

I thought I was for it, but she just said, 'I'd always imagined you as more of a handlebar moustache type of girl.'

And that was it. It's nice to see that at least one person managed to slip through that ban on teachers with a sense of humour.

LATER

Unlike Miss Ramsbottom, who lectured me and Lily without so much as a hint of a smile. Then we had to scrub our upper lips. Which, as I said to Lily, was fairly pointless because we just ended up with red tashes instead of black ones.

When I told Megs about it in Maths she said, 'It's good that you're having fun with Lily.' But she didn't really sound that enthusiastic.

FRIDAY 9TH SEPTEMBER

At lunchtime I went to meet Megs. Lily and shorty-pants Angharad came too. When Lily first made friends with Angharad, some nasty girls started calling them 'the Welsh one and the weird one'. It took Lily a whole term to notice and when she did she asked me why people thought she was Welsh. Angharad is definitely the brains of that duo.

Since I've been in my new tutor group, I've discovered that Angharad is as sweet as she is small. She looks about nine, but she can't help that, so I try to only mention it once or twice a day.

The corner of the cafeteria where Megs and I hung out last year has been taken over by the Year Eleven Tarty Party. They all wear too much orange makeup, and pluck their eyebrows till they disappear and then draw them back on too high up, so they look really surprised. I wanted to have it out with them, but Megs said it wasn't worth it and Angharad started shaking at the thought of a confrontation.

I scowled at the Tarty Party from across the room and said, 'I don't know why they bother to keep coming to school anyway; they're not learning anything. It's as much as they can do to point at things and name them.'

Just then one of the tarts spotted me looking at her and she jabbed a finger at me and called out, 'Ginger!'

'See,' I said, 'just like toddlers.'

Then the queen tart threw a plastic fork at Angharad and shouted, 'Sheep-lover!'

Being mean to Angharad is like stomping on a kitten. I wanted to smack the tart, but Megs dragged me away and we went to hang out under the trees outside instead.

I said, 'They're so rude. How would they like it if I pointed at them and called them thick and ugly?'

Megs said, 'You do call them that.'

'Yes, but like, if I said it to their faces.'

'You do say it to their faces.'

'Shut up, Megs. I'm not the one stealing other people's lunch space.'

'I don't think you can stop them sitting there,' Angharad said. 'That table hasn't got your name on it.'

Megs said, 'Actually, it has. Faith wrote it on the underside with a glitter pen last term.'

I was going to give them all a lecture on how we shouldn't let the Tarty Party push us around and how we should unite our year together against the Evil Oranges to ensure that we have the freedom to sit where we like, but then I spotted that Lily had a packet of Giant Chocolate Buttons so I stopped talking and started chomping – you know, just to help her keep down her sugar intake for the day. I'm always thinking of others.

SATURDAY 10TH SEPTEMBER

I don't know why, perhaps it's the plucky way I continue to believe in human kindness, but I thought it would be a good idea to share my musical ambitions with the bunch of losers who hang around my house and claim to have some kind of genetic link to me. Dad just started laughing and my freak little brother said, 'A choir? Oh yes, that's where they put the people who aren't good enough to perform solo, isn't it?'

So I said, 'A concrete-filled box? Oh yes, that's where they put the brothers who don't deserve to live, isn't it?'

Then Mum wafted in reading her astrology magazine and said, 'What a grim image, Faith. Can't we start the day with something more uplifting?'

Sam smirked and said, 'Faith is already uplifted. She's wearing a push-up bra.'

So then I wrestled him to the floor and jammed my knee in his throat.

Mum was right. It is nice to start the day with something uplifting.

SUNDAY 11TH SEPTEMBER

Megs came round so we could talk about our dire situation. I wanted to discuss ways to punish Miss Ramsbottom for splitting us up, but Megs had her own ideas (even though I'm always telling her not to). She says that we should be really well-behaved to make Ramsbottom think we have reformed our ways.

I said, 'Megan, I don't know why you think I've got a vacancy for another person telling me to be good, but I haven't. If you're looking for a job with me, I can offer you drinks waitress or chief polisher of my shoes instead.'

Megs gave me a stern look. 'How are you getting along in 10SW?'

'It's all right.' The truth is that even though Lily is delightfully mad and Angharad is cute, I am missing Megs.

'Have you done your startled beetle impression yet?'

I mumbled.

'Did anyone laugh? No? I didn't think so.'

'Yeah, well—'

'And I know you think Lily is all that . . .'

'What do you mean, "all that"?'

'. . . But I bet she can't do your mum's signature so you don't have to do PE and you've got no one to translate what that Australian teaching assistant is saying, have you? You're lost with me, aren't you?'

'A bit.'

'Let's face it, Faith, without me you're going to wither and die.'

'Oh, it's true!' I said. 'I can't take it, Megs. 10SW is mostly full of swots who don't even know any good poo jokes. What are we going to do?'

'I'll tell you what we're going to do.' Megs was getting a bit of a crazy look in her eyes. This is what happens when I let her have her own way, but I'll have to worry about getting her back under my thumb later because what she was saying did make sense. For once.

'You are going to *behave*,' she said grimly. 'You are going to be on time, you're going to do your homework, you're going to say polite things to your classmates and you're going to smile at teachers.'

'Steady on, Megs, I don't want them locking me up for obvious insanity.'

'If we want to get you away from 10SW then these are the kind of sacrifices you're going to have to make.'

She may have extracted a promise from me. But since she dragged it out of me by dangling a KitKat under my nose I don't think it's legally binding. But I do need to get back to Megs. She is a turnip, but she is *my* turnip so I will give this crazy good behaviour business a go.

MONDAY 12TH SEPTEMBER

I have kept my word to Megs and been angelic all day. Well there was a little bit of fun in Maths, but nothing serious.

Megs and I were talking about our first choir rehearsal with the boys. (It's this Friday, so we don't have much time to prepare.) Becky and Zoe who sit in front of us in Maths have signed up too. During class, Zoe (who loves to speak her mind, i.e. to say something nasty) pointed a finger at me and said, 'But you can't really sing, can you, Faith?'

Which is nonsense. I just haven't got a traditional

sort of voice. I said, 'What do you mean, I *can't really* sing?'

'Well, I mean you can't sing at all.'

I gave her a hard stare.

'It's just that everyone else there is going to be experienced and trained and, you know . . . not awful.'

'So what you're saying is that I am going to be surrounded by voices from heaven?'

'Uh-huh.'

'Who the monkey do you think is going to notice my unconventional tone then?'

'Maybe just those people who have *ears*.'

'I'll mime.'

Zoe seems to have forgotten my obvious acting talent. For example I did an amazing performance last year as the stomach in our mid-Biology-lesson show, *What happens to things we eat?* The girls who played the food really did look partially digested when I had finished with them. Despite this, Zoe seems to think I lack the skills to pull off a bit of lip-syncing. So to prove her wrong I moved my lips while Megs talked for the rest of the lesson. Admittedly, Mrs Baxter did call us 'a pair of silly beggars', but not before we had got away with Megs answering three questions about fractions through me. It was only when she got the giggles and made me mouth the words to 'Little Bo Peep' that we were busted.

I mean, how can I be expected to behave myself when I get provoked into things like that?

TUESDAY 13TH SEPTEMBER

Chucked it down with rain today, which meant we couldn't sit under the trees at lunchtime. I was struck with a stroke of genius and Megs and I went to the sports hall. (I wanted to bring Angharad and Lily too, but Megs didn't look keen when I suggested it, so I didn't ask them.) Once we had shuffled past some insane Year Sevens who were practising formation skipping *in their own time* we slipped into the gym equipment cupboard.

Three crash mats in a pile is actually not an uncomfortable place for a lunchtime snooze.

WEDNESDAY 14TH SEPTEMBER

Granny came round this evening. I told Mum that I would be busy with homework and wouldn't be available to have my fingernails criticised. But ever since Miss Ramsbottom rang my crumbly parents to discuss my tutor group move, Mum and Dad have decided that it's good for me to have them tell me what to do.

'You'll stay and be uplifted by some quality inter-generational family time,' Mum said.

Which meant sitting still while Granny told me what's wrong with the youth of today. Eventually she paused. She didn't do it on purpose; it was because she was choking on her false teeth. While she was hooking them out I decided to tell her what's wrong with the old people of today. I started with Miss Ramsbottom. Surprisingly, Granny seemed quite interested. She even told me to stand up for myself.

I asked, 'What did you do with teachers you didn't like?'

'Put frogs in their beds and porridge in their wellingtons.'

'Thanks, Granny. Next time Miss Ramsbottom annoys me on a day when we slip through a time warp to a girls' boarding school in the nineteen-twenties I'll make sure that I use that advice.'

Granny has dyed her hair again. She used to be chestnut-brown, but now she is bright blonde.

I said, 'Your hair looks very . . . young, Granny.' Which seemed to please her.

She said, 'Oh, yes, my hair always gets blonder in the summer.'

Yeah, right. Why is it that when I tell a teeny white lie my mother tells me that if I send dishonesty out into the universe I'll get dishonesty right back, but when Granny tells a whopper like that we just have to smile and nod?

Anyway, I think Sam scored a point for the side of truth when he came bounding into the room and said, 'I like your wig, Granny.'

Ha. Granny didn't flinch though, she just said, 'Raymond says I look like a film star.'

I said, 'Is he the one who lost his eyes during the war?'

'Faith, I'm too young to know anything about the war and you're thinking of Oscar, who lost an eye in a knife fight in the jungle.'

It's so embarrassing when your grandmother has more boyfriends than you do. She spent the rest of the evening talking about them. I think she's got enough for a football team now.

After Granny had gone I noticed that the new packet of Penguins was missing from the biscuit tin, even though I never saw her go to the kitchen. That woman is a biscuit-stealing ninja.

THURSDAY 15TH SEPTEMBER

Rang Megs to discuss what we will wear at the rehearsal tomorrow.

'We'll have to wear uniform, Faith. It's straight after last lesson,' Megs said.

'We could change. You'd be surprised how quickly I can get into a nice outfit in an emergency. Once, I was in the garden in my trackies when I spotted a fit boy cutting next-door's hedge; by the time he turned round I was in hot pants.'

'*Everybody* will be in uniform.'

'It's not a uniform, it's a fabric force field guaranteed to repel all boys. And it's *bottle green*.'

'It's all right for you, you've got ginger hair.'

'*Auburn*, my hair is auburn, not ginger, Megan, and what has that got to do with it?'

'Redheads can wear green. It makes you look like something out of an Irish fairytale.'

'Are you calling me a leprechaun?'

'I'm just saying you look better than I do. What kind of sicko designed our uniform anyway?'

I thought for a moment. 'Megs, I can think of only one group of people who would want teenage girls to look so hideous. It has to be their fathers.'

In the end, I've decided to improve my uniform by wearing opaque black tights for leg lengthening effect. And my black patent kitten heels for kittening effect. And obviously my push-up bra.

It's not that I've got no chest, it's just that it all needs rounding up and pointing in the right direction, otherwise it could get lost under my jumper. But at least I've got something. It could be worse, I could be as flat-chested as Zoe, who went and had a seriously ill-thought-out cropped hairdo last term. When she went to the inter-schools hockey championship, the St Mildred's PE teacher took one look at Zoe and said, 'We don't play mixed-sex teams.'

Which just goes to show. Sport doesn't pay.

LATER

I tried to pack the necessaries (kitten heels, spare tights, deodorant, perfume, toothbrush, artist's case of makeup etc.) in my school bag, but I couldn't get everything to fit, so I took out the other junk (Maths textbook, contact book, badly-made packed lunch suggesting I am a neglected child – why have I got a hippy for a mother? Nobody else is expected to last through double Physics in the afternoon after just some bean sprout mix and a handwritten horoscope). Anyway, everything fits in now. Except the makeup.

I'll just have to wear it all.

FRIDAY 16TH SEPTEMBER

Ooh la la. What an awesome day.

When we got to the hall for rehearsals the first thing I noticed was Vicky Blundell (Year Ten's biggest bimbo and 'affectionately' known as Icky to me and my friends). She was flexing her metre-long false nails and circling the boys like a vulture. A vulture with its skirt rolled over till you could practically see its vulture knickers. And we all know those are the worst kind.

The chairs were still out from assembly and all the girls seemed to be sitting on the right-hand side and all the boys on the left. Except boys don't sit. They loll. And lounge. And sort of sprawl over about three chairs and rest their massive trainered feet on anything available – their bag, the piano, each other's head ... Anyway, I was horrified (not by the feet, it would be hard for them to hold themselves up if they just had stumps) by this boy/girl divide. What was everybody thinking? How were we going to meet anybody interesting (i.e. male) if we were on opposite sides of the room? There they were, all the younger girls, looking at their music and humming under their breath, and not even trying a bit of eyelash fluttering. It was almost as if they had come there to sing!

Then the Year Elevens arrived. They certainly weren't shy and all available seats on the boys' side started filling up. I panicked and desperately looked for space, pulling Megs along. Then I saw Icky Blundell again, with a large pack of boys on one side and two empty chairs on the other. I don't know what came over me. I said, 'Vicky! Thanks for saving us seats.'

Icky looked me up and down and said, 'There are only two chairs. Where's your backside going to sit?'

What a cow. Just because she's about two foot nine and her scrawny behind would fit into a teacup.

I said, 'I know my healthy proportions must be intimidating, Vicky. I've been meaning to ask you about your rickets. Did you not get any sunlight as a child because your parents were too ashamed to take you outside?'

Megs elbowed me in the ribs. Three boys sat in front of us had turned around and were staring at me.

One of them said, 'Wow, I'd hate to see what you'd say to someone who hadn't saved you a seat.'

We chatted to the boys for the rest of the rehearsal (except when Mr Millet rudely interrupted to say things like, 'Open the back of your throat' and, 'Now try it in tune' and, 'If I have to speak to you one more time, girl-with-the-red-hair . . .'). The one that spoke to us first is called Ethan. He's got dark, curly hair and quite good eyes. (Good to look *at* rather than to look with. Although, I'm assuming that they work well enough because he didn't trip over anything.) Ethan's friends are Cameron (who has spiky, brown hair and a cheeky grin) and Elliot (who, quite frankly, is a bit on the titchy side of small). Elliot didn't say much, but Ethan and Cameron were both quite funny. I could tell that Megs was really into Cameron. Straight away she started tossing her head about so much that I had to keep fishing her hair out of my mouth.

Icky Blundell tried to get in on the conversation a few times, but I was pleased to see that the boys didn't seem to think much of her.

At one point Icky turned to Ethan and said, 'I'm here because Mr Millet invited me especially. He says I've got a unique voice.'

Ethan just looked at her and said, 'I'm here because my social worker says I've got to learn to mix with other teenagers and stop taking my homicidal rage out on girls with false nails.'

Fantastic. Disliking Icky is quite near the top of my list of requirements in a boy. I think these rehearsals are going to be fun.

SATURDAY 17TH SEPTEMBER

My parents seem to think that just because I have vowed to impress people with my cheerful and cooperative attitude at school that they can expect the same sort of thing at home. When am I supposed to rest? When do I get time to be the real me?

Mum's latest unfair demand is that I tidy my room. I said, 'Why?'

'Clutter in the house clutters the mind. I don't want to see that kind of chaos every time I walk past your room.'

'I could close the door.'

'I want your room tidy by lunchtime.'

'Doesn't all this ordering me about go against your hippy principles? Shouldn't you allow me ownership of my personal space and let me develop my sense of order in my own time?'

'I think we'd be waiting a long time if we did that, don't you?'

What I think is that my mum only sticks to her flower-power philosophy when it suits her. I didn't say that out loud because she often gets quite shirty when faced with the truth, so instead I said, 'Why *are* you a hippy, Mum? Have you really got no sense of style or do you genuinely like tie-dye?'

She rolled her eyes, but then she smiled and I thought I might have hit on a good distraction technique. 'Shall I tell you a secret?' she asked.

I nodded.

'To be honest, when I was young being a hippy was something I got into because it annoyed your granny. You know what conservative views she's got. Talking about peace and free love was an easy way to wind her up.'

'Are you telling me that you've eaten lentils and worn those terrible tasselled skirts for all these years just to irritate Granny? Wow. I am a much better daughter than you; when I do something deliberately to annoy you, I only keep it up for a day or two. A month at the most.'

'No, Faith! I didn't keep it up just to get Granny's goat. My beliefs are very important to me. And hippies are good people. Just look at the lovely women we met at that cooperative in the summer.

They were so relaxed and friendly. People like that don't judge.'

'I don't know about that, I got a pretty vicious look when I put a Marmite jar in the green glass recycling bin.'

'Yes, well they've got strong views on that sort of thing and so have I. Don't you think it's vital to preserve the planet for you and all the other children that will come after you?'

'Yes,' I said. 'I do think we should take care of the environment, I really do.'

'Right then, we can start with the home environment. Get tidying.'

If there was ever any doubt as to where I get my evil genius from, I think it's just been cleared up.

LATER

So here I am, tidying.

I am so bored.

If they had hired me a maid for my birthday, like I asked, none of this would be necessary.

AFTER LUNCH

I'm finished. My mess will no longer disturb the delicate balance of my mother's mind.

As long as she doesn't look in my wardrobe.

Or under my bed.

SUNDAY 18TH SEPTEMBER

Granny was supposed to come for lunch today, but she didn't turn up, even though I had prepared for her by spending the morning cleaning out the biscuit tin. She's probably out with one of her boyfriends.

LATER

Mum wanted to know why I couldn't manage my lunch.

I told her that's what three orange Clubs, four chocolate fingers and half a custard cream will do to you.

MONDAY 19TH SEPTEMBER

About a million years ago, a conversation took place that must have gone something like this:

Careers advisor: So, young lady, what would you say your key skills are?

Girl: I'm mean, I'm petty, and I particularly dislike girls with red hair for no good reason.

Careers advisor: And do you think you could falsely accuse young people of misbehaving?

Girl: At fifty paces with my eyes closed.

Careers advisor: Welcome to the world of teaching.

Yes, Miss Ramsbottom has struck again. First, she bellowed at me down the corridor to stop behaving like a monkey. I don't think a lady with freaktacular long arms like hers is in a position to make ape jokes. And what's wrong with a little between-lessons swinging on the swing doors? Surely it's good for my health? I told her this politely, but firmly, 'I'm fighting off childhood obesity, Miss Ramsbottom.'

But she has no sense of humour and made me go to her classroom to clean her whiteboard. Which, as a punishment, is pretty poor, especially since there's a lovely swingy door right outside her classroom.

I'm just saying.

LATER

Megs was cross with me for getting into trouble with Miss Ramsbottom, but as I pointed out, Miss R had obviously had an extra-large bowl of Scornflakes this morning and everyone was finding it hard to stay out of trouble with her. At lunchtime I saw her yank out one of the Tarty Party's fake ponytail and during year assembly she made Lily look really stupid. To be fair to Miss Ramsbottom it's not hard to make Lily look stupid, in fact I once did it accidentally just by asking her to hold out her left hand, but I think it was rather unnecessary to haul Lily up in front of the whole year just because she didn't think through trying to boil water in a plastic beaker during our Science lesson.

To cap it all, in between harassing us, Miss Ramsbottom was swanking about with yet another lush new handbag, but as I have just said to Lily on the phone, 'She should spend some of her handbag fund on electrolysis. Did you see her tash today?'

'Yes, I think it quivered with delight when she made everyone laugh at me.'

'Not everyone laughed at you, Lily.'

'Oh! You are such a good mate, Faith.'

Actually, I meant Hazel Hunt didn't laugh. Although, that may have been because she has had her jaw wired. Her mother won't let her be a bridesmaid unless she loses two stone. But I'm sure she wouldn't have laughed anyway. Nothing's very funny when all you can think about is whether you can liquidise a Big Mac and suck it through a straw.

Anyway, I am not happy about Miss Ramsbottom terrorising people like this. I don't care what promises I made to Megs under the influence of chocolate deprivation, if Ramsbottom keeps this up then I shall have to do something about it.

TUESDAY 20TH SEPTEMBER

Icky Blundell has got a boyfriend! Incredible! I don't remember her actually talking to any of the boys at the rehearsal. She just kept smirking and swinging her spindly legs around. But apparently, after the rehearsal a whole group of girls went to McDonald's with a load of the boys. I spent most of the day trying to find out who was in this 'whole group', but it seems like it was mostly Year Elevens and Icky Blundell. I can't understand why the top year girls let her hang around. I don't know how she does it, but people seem to think that Icky is fun and pretty. *Why?*

The boyfriend is called Dan and he's in Year Eleven. He must be desperate.

I rang Megs to ask for some helpful insight. 'Do you find Icky Blundell attractive?'

'Faith, I'm not going to give an answer now, because it's possible that one day I will wake up as a balding troll and then I will be grateful for the love of Ms Blundell.'

'Fair point, but if you were to be turned into a human boy instead of a balding troll, do you think you would find her attractive?'

'The thing about Vicky is that *she* thinks she's attractive and that seems to convince everyone else.'

'Surely it can't be that simple? I mean I firmly believe that I am a model student but that's never convinced Miss Ramsbottom, has it?'

'Anyway, Zoe's sister says this Dan is fit-ish and not utterly thick.'

'Maybe he's got back acne.'

'Thanks, Faith, I'll use that happy thought to get me to sleep.'

LATER

Now that I think about it, Megs was a bit odd on the phone. We had only chatted for a very short hour and a half then, when I wanted to tell her about Lily juggling shoes in History, suddenly Megs said she had to go. In fact, every time I mention Lily, Megs is weird. I don't know why, they've always got on before.

WEDNESDAY 21ST SEPTEMBER

I can't stop thinking about Icky. It seems so unfair that she has got a love life when I haven't. I've been day-dreaming about Ethan asking me to be his girlfriend and Cameron asking Megs out and then we could all go somewhere really cool on a date. Then we could all get cast in a new reality TV series and live together in a loft apartment in London with a butler.

That would be nice.

Or I would settle for Dan publicly dumping Icky. That would be nice too.

THURSDAY 22ND SEPTEMBER

Dan was waiting for Icky at the gates. I knew it was him by the way she wiggled her way towards him and then attached herself to his mouth. I don't think she even said hello. It's not that I wanted to see Icky kissing, but I couldn't help looking. It's a bit like when you drive past a car crash. It's pretty sick to stare, but it's strangely compelling. Besides, I need to watch other people kiss, otherwise how will I know what to do when I finally get some lip action myself? I can't believe I'm fourteen and I've never been kissed.

I wonder if Miss Ramsbottom has got a boyfriend. What a scary thought. Kissing Miss Ramsbottom probably turns you to stone. I reckon her house is full of statues of poor frozen blokes. I bet she lures in pizza delivery boys with her long legs and her expensive perfume and then she pounces.

I don't think Icky was paralysing Dan. In fact, he seemed to be melting. He was sweaty and there was drool around his chin. They didn't move much either. They were just locked together.

To be honest, it looked a bit dull. If I'd been Icky I'd have been tempted to flick open a magazine behind his head.

FRIDAY 23RD SEPTEMBER

Megs and I got to the rehearsal early so we could save seats for Ethan, Cameron and Elliot. While we were waiting for them Lily arrived and I waved her over. Megs rolled her eyes so I said, 'What? I thought you liked Lily. At my birthday party last year you two got on like a house on fire.'

She sniffed, 'Yeah, well, we didn't use to spend quite so much time with her.'

I need to have a chat with Megs about this stroppiness.

The Radcliffe boys arrived and Ethan and co had just sat down with us when in walked the best-looking boy I have ever seen. He was tanned and had that messy blond I've-just-been-surfing hair down to his collar. He looked like someone from an Australian soap. Or like someone in a boy band – the lead singer of a boy band, not the slightly podgy one or the one with strange teeth that they always put at the back of the photo.

So, he walked in. What a walk. I didn't know walking could be so impressive. He strode along with a bunch of mates and everyone turned to look at him. Even Icky took her tongue out of Dan's ear for a minute.

Megs said, 'Who. Is. That?'

Ethan rolled his eyes, 'Finn Ryland.'

I said, 'Why wasn't he here last week?'

'I expect he was getting his highlights done,' Ethan replied.

Cameron butted in, 'Actually, he was still on holiday in the States.'

Ethan went on, 'Oh, so the hairdressers in this country aren't good enough for him?'

Which made me laugh, although this Finn doesn't look like one of those horribly vain boys who spend hours making sure the points of their gelled hair are all the same height. In fact, there's a kind of scruffiness about his loveliness. He looks like he just fell out of bed looking that gorgeous.

Not only is Finn incredible-looking, he is also an amazing singer. He's got a solo part in three of the songs we're doing – I can't remember which ones; they all sound the same to me. I must try and pay attention, so when I manage to wangle a chat with him I've got something intelligent to say.

Angharad was unusually quiet at the rehearsal. I mean, she's always quiet, but today she was so quiet that halfway through the rehearsal I said, 'Where's Angharad disappeared to?'

And Lily pointed out that she was stood next to me and had been for half an hour.

I said, 'Come on, Ang! Speak up. Mr Millet loves it when we interrupt his long and boring instructions with our witty chat. I'll be getting worried about you if you don't give us a little mousy squeak at least once a day. Are you all right?'

And she said, 'Yes.'

After a while I realised that she was taking a great interest in the chair in front of her. And then I wondered if she was interested in the contents of the chair, namely, titchy Elliot. I looked at Ang, then I looked Elliot and I said in a discreet fashion, 'Woooooo! Ang! You love Elliot!'

Angharad seemed ridiculously annoyed by my friendly interest in her love life, which was silly because as I was voicing my matey concern a boy called Westy was making farting noises with both armpits simultaneously, so no one heard except Angharad. (And maybe two or three rows behind us. Four or five max.) Even though I explained this, Angharad displayed an aggressive side I have never seen before. Not only did she say, 'Shhh, Faith!' She also *tutted*. Yes, she was that angry. But as I said to Lily and some other girls I've never met before, Angharad's secret is safe with me. I will tell no one that she lurves Elliot.

At the end of the rehearsal I thought I should do something to boost my own love opportunities, so Megs and I tried to sort of happen to end up near super-fit Finn while he was packing up his music. Unfortunately, all the rest of the girls were trying to sort of happen to end up next to him too, so there was a gridlock situation until Westy yelled, 'Ferret!' and all the girls ran, screaming.

SATURDAY 24TH SEPTEMBER

I'm bored.

I told Dad and he suggested that I 'play with Sam'. It's sad the way he ignores my blossoming womanhood so that he can pretend I'm still seven.

LATER

On the other hand, he's given me an idea. Sam is still good for a bit of entertainment one way or another.

SUNDAY 25TH SEPTEMBER

Today I was forced to go to Granny's house.

I said to Mum, 'If you're trying to punish me for Sam's hair, couldn't I just go to church instead?'

Personally, I don't think I should be punished for what happened yesterday. If Sam's stupid enough to believe someone when they say that Golden Syrup is a 'great styling product' then he deserves what he gets.

Mum said, 'This isn't about punishment, Faith. It's about family. Your grandmother is a part of our family. She also has the wisdom of age. You should respect that.'

'I could go to the Russian Orthodox church? They make you stand for three hours in there.'

But no, I had to go to Granny's. I don't know why Mum was defending her. She wasn't so keen on Granny's elderly wisdom when Granny told her that she read in the *Daily Mail* that being a vegetarian makes your teeth fall out.

When we arrived, Granny inhaled the shortbread we'd taken her and then talked us through her ongoing battle with the neighbours over who puts their recycling bin where. She had the cheek to finish with a yawn. 'I was out late with Geoff,' she said, then she turned her laser eyes on me and said, 'I hope you're not out every night with boys. Has she got a boyfriend? Have you got a boyfriend?'

I thought this was going to be one of those conversations Granny has where you're not allowed to join in, so it took me a while to realise that she'd actually asked me a question.

I said, 'No.'

'Well, we can't all be the belle of the ball. Of course when I was your age I was practically married.'

'Really, Granny? How old were you when you got married?'

'Twenty.'

Which made me think that either the old girl isn't very good at maths, or she was imagining that I was a bit older than I am. I thought I might as well take advantage of this so I said, 'That's nice. Can I have a gin, Granny?'

She wasn't listening, but I'm definitely trying that one again at Christmas.

Then Mum thought it would be nice to look at Granny's photo albums. The old ones are full of my parents' wedding day and rubbish like that, but the most recent one is jam-packed with pictures of Granny on different holidays with different men. Granny couldn't remember all of their names, but she could remember other details. She jabbed her finger across the page saying: 'Pilot, dentist, company director, millionaire, diamond thief, King of Spain.' (I might have made the last couple up, but the point is that Granny is very shallow and really only interested in rich men. Not like me. I don't care how much money they've got. I value what really counts in a relationship, like true love and sun-streaked hair.)

While I was looking at a photo of Granny in Blackpool with a man who she said was 'very big in the plastic cutlery business', she asked again, 'Have you got a boyfriend?'

If she's going to forget things, why couldn't she do something useful twice? Like slip me a tenner.

I said, 'Well, it's hard to choose. There are two nice young men who are battling it out for my affections.'

'Goodness! Well you know what to do in that situation, don't you dear?'

'No, what should I do?'

'Find out what their fathers do. I don't want a coal miner in the family.'

And that's the wisdom of age for you.

LATER

On the way home we stopped at the twenty-four-hour supermarket 'as a treat'. Seriously, that's what my dad said.

I may as well have gone to school today.

MONDAY 26TH SEPTEMBER

I have just discovered that Icky is doing a duet with Finn at the concert. I said to Megs, 'Why? What has she got that I haven't?'

'Perfect pitch?'

'Don't tell me that the poisonous pixie can sing?'

'Faith, you knew that. Don't you remember last year when we had to listen to her warbling at the carol service?'

'Megs, when I step inside a church I enter a deep state of calm and I am oblivious to the bustle around me.'

'You mean you slept through it.'

'There's no need to say it like it's a bad thing. It was for her own good, if you look at Icky when she's showing off it only encourages her.'

'Yeah, well I'm afraid that she's pretty good.'

44

'She might be good, but she's not pretty. I think the best solution for all concerned would be for her to sing from the wings and I'll stand next to Finn and mime.'

'Is mime your solution to everything?'

'Actually, I've got a whole range of problem-solving strategies. As well as mime, I also use water pistols and dirty looks.'

TUESDAY 27TH SEPTEMBER

I have been behaving my socks off and no one seems to have noticed. I haven't so much as set off a single explosion, but I still haven't been moved back with Megs. It's true that I am spectacularly popular with 10SW and everyone was clamouring to sit next to me in Geography today (I chose Lily, but it honestly had very little to do with the fact that she was packing three tubes of Rolos), but the thing is that still I feel lost without my Megs. I miss our chats. I miss the way that I would say something quite rude but funny about her and then she would say something quite rude but funny back. No one else seems capable of having a proper conversation like that. If you say something rude to Angharad she cries. If you say something a bit cheeky to Zoe she wraps your ponytail around your neck. And it doesn't really matter what you say to Lily, you'll end up having to look at the smiley faces she's painted on her toenails anyway.

Basically, it's hard work getting some decent conversation at the moment.

After school I rang up Megs to tell how much I love and appreciate her.

I said, 'Hello, Fatty, I think you've put on some weight. It's probably because you are not getting the usual stimulating workout from trying to keep up with me both physically and mentally.'

She said, 'If you weren't such an imbecile you wouldn't have got us into this mess in the first place.'

It was nice to have a heart-to-heart with my bestie.

Later on, I started wondering whether we are going about this the right way. All this exhausting good behaviour doesn't seem to be getting us anywhere. Maybe I'm not the problem, maybe what we need to do is get rid of Miss Ramsbottom.

I'm just saying.

WEDNESDAY 28TH SEPTEMBER

Someone set off the fire alarm today. Luckily it was during PSHE, so we didn't miss anything that we'll need to know about in the real world.

10NM were in the middle of getting changed for PE, which meant we were treated to Icky Blundell in her underwear (funny how everybody else managed to fling on some clothes). Anyone else might have been embarrassed to be caught out in their knick-knocks, but Icky cartwheeled over to her friend in 10LV to cadge a lollipop and twirled about like the Sugar Plum Scary. Then she met up with the popular crew in Year Eleven and talked about what they're going to wear on Saturday night. Unbelievable. Meanwhile I was spending my time sensibly by asking Megs if she knew the answers to the work we were doing in PSHE. I was also keeping up my energy for learning with a few of Lily's Dolly Mixtures. Lily offered them to Megs, but she said no.

When we were marching back into school I said to Megs, 'Why are you being funny with Lily? I know she's bonkers, but she's pretty funny really and she's generous with her sweets and—'

'Yes, I know, you're a *big fan*. Listen, Faith, we're two individuals and we're not always going to like the same people. And that's fine. We can have our own friends, can't we?'

Which all sounded very sensible and mature, but to be honest I wanted to stamp my foot and say, 'Like my friend!' But I didn't. I pouted and said, 'I s'pose so.'

THURSDAY 29TH SEPTEMBER
Miss Pee asked us in assembly today if anyone knew anything about the fire alarm going off.

I don't think it's surprising that we all looked at Icky.

FRIDAY 30TH SEPTEMBER

Our group at the rehearsal has expanded. Zoe and Becky have started sitting with us and so have a few more of Ethan's mates. Some of the boys are a bit stupid. Especially Westy.

I asked Ethan, 'Is he really called Westy?'

'Nah. His name is Scott West. Boys just like sticking an "o" or a "y" on the end of people's names.'

'He's quite . . . full on, isn't he?'

'Westy's all right.'

Which is not how I would describe him. See, I think Zoe is all right. She's chatty, she laughs at my jokes, she has an acceptable level of personal hygiene and I'm sure she would lend me her mascara in an emergency. Whereas, Westy is sweaty, farty and shouty. Every time he gets to the end of a sentence he whacks somebody over the head to celebrate managing to string so many words together.

Fit Finn is not at all like Westy. Westy is constantly hyper, whereas Finn is super-laid-back. He was practising one of his solos today, so we all got to have a good stare. His skin is so brown and his hair is so golden, he looks like some sort of beach angel. I think I'd be a bit nervous about singing in front of a hall full of people, but Finn didn't seem bothered. He just strolled up to the front and then this incredible voice powered out of him. Amazing.

Later on Mr Millet asked Finn to hand out some new music. With a little elbowing and one swift poke in the eye to Icky, I managed to get to the end of the line, which meant that Finn handed me the sheets for our row. Our hands brushed and I said, 'Thanks.'

He said, 'No problem.'

I think we really connected.

I'm not one to think only of myself, though. At the beginning of the rehearsal, by some subtle manoeuvring I managed to make sure that Angharad sat next to Elliot. (I said, 'Westy, you great lump, don't sit there, Angharad wants to be near her pocket prince.') Angharad turned plum-coloured, which I think was a sign of joy. The happy couple didn't say a word to each other until the very end, when Elliot looked at Ang's shoes and said, 'Are you going to be here next week?'

Angharad gave the tiniest nod and her blushing reached nuclear levels.

Ahh. I have brought them together.

LATER

Wait a minute, not, '*Ahh*'. Why is no one checking that I will be there next week? Finn walked past me at the end as if our hands had never touched and Ethan only raised his eyebrows at me as he left.

Mind you, Westy did have him in a headlock at the time so it must have been quite an effort.

OCTOBER

SATURDAY 1ST OCTOBER

Megs has been dribbling on about Cameron since yesterday without drawing breath. I hung up the phone at half ten last night and when I called her this morning she was still gushing and sighing. I'm not sure she noticed I was gone in between. After three hours of talking we had drawn two conclusions: Cameron is quite nice and he doesn't seem to dislike Megs.

I said, 'What are you going to do next? If you like him you should take it further.'

'Don't know. I could flirt with him.'

'How will you do that?'

'Flick my hair?'

'You've done enough of that and you'll find it hard to snog him if you've got whiplash. Why don't you ask him out?'

'Because, Faith, I'm not insane. I just need to spend some more time around him and work out if he likes me.'

'You know the Radcliffe boys sometimes go into town at lunchtime. We could go.'

'We're not supposed to go out of school grounds during the day.'

'Megs, we're not supposed to make the supply teachers cry, but that's never stopped us.'

'OK, on Monday let's go boy-spotting.'

'Whoa, not Monday. Better make it Tuesday.

I've got PE Monday morning. No boy is going to be attracted to me with a shiny red face. And if they are, then they're a bit strange and I'm not really interested.'

Finally, we got to talk about more important things, i.e. is Ethan helplessly attracted to me?

Yesterday at the rehearsal when I went to drink from my sports bottle of water, someone had loosened the cap, so instead of sipping gracefully from the spout I sloshed water all down my front. Westy and Ethan laughed their heads off. Actually everyone laughed their heads off, but Westy punched Ethan in the back and said, 'Nice one.' So I'm assuming Ethan was the culprit.

I asked Megs, 'What do you think it means?'

'I thought you liked Finn.'

'My granny says it doesn't hurt to have a spare. Tell me what you think Ethan mucking about with my water bottle means?'

'Maybe he was trying to drown you.'

'You know, Megan, I have just spent my entire morning thinking of reasons why everything Cameron does means he fancies you, it would be good manners if you did the same thing back.'

'Sorry. Perhaps it means he fancies you?'

'Why does it?'

'I don't know. I'm just saying it because you told me to say it.'

At that point I told her to call me back after she'd been to sit on the stairs and thought about what she'd done.

Eventually the phone rang.

Megs said, 'My mum says that when boys like you they tease you and pull your hair and stuff and that maybe pouring water over you is like that.'

'Hmm. That's interesting. What am I supposed to do?'

'Mum said that you should tease him back.'

'I should play a trick on him? That's what flirting is all about? Why did nobody say so before? I think I'm a natural.'

'Do you want to do something this afternoon?' Megs asked.

'That depends. Have you learnt from your poor behaviour? Or shall I ask your mum round to try on makeup instead of you?'

SUNDAY 2ND OCTOBER

I spent this morning thinking about tricks and practical jokes I could play on Ethan.

I thought I'd have a little practice on Sam. But he failed to fall for my plastic biscuit or my water-squirting ring. I got a bit annoyed then.

So I tripped him up.

Sometimes the classics are the funniest.

MONDAY 3RD OCTOBER

Lovely day. Mrs Macready showed us a pig's heart in Biology. At the beginning of the lesson she asked if anyone felt uncomfortable with dissection. I didn't have any objections. That old pig was already dead for sausages and I think it's nice that we're using his heart to learn about the wonder of Biology, especially when you think about what could have happened to it. For example, Miss Ramsbottom (or any other practising witch) could have bought it to suck the blood out of.

Angharad obviously didn't realise that the pig was fulfilling his higher purpose. She put up a limp hand and managed to get out the word, 'vegetarian'.

I said, 'It's all right, Ang, she doesn't want you to eat it.'

Angharad put her hand over her mouth, and that got me hoping that we might be in for some projectile vomiting so I added, 'You've just got to slice it up into chunks.'

At which point Mrs Mac said that Angharad could wait outside. Poor old Ang didn't know what to do. She can't bear to be away from her education. Once, Icky Blundell jammed a compass into the back of Ang's wrist in the middle of a Maths test. Ang was too weak to pull it out, but she didn't tell anyone till she'd finished her test. With her left hand.

Clearly the idea of missing twenty minutes of Biology was too much to bear because she gritted her teeth and told Mrs Mac she would stay.

So we gathered round the front desk, with me at the front, and the butchering began. I think it's probably for the best that Mrs Mac ended up wasting her life teaching, because if she'd made it as a doctor she would have been involved in endless court cases. The lady is not great with a knife. She sort of stabbed about saying things like, 'Och, that's a gristly bit'. She reminded me of Granny eating her dinner. She did try to show us some points of interest, but it's not like in the book where everything is neatly labelled. I grabbed Angharad from the back of the crowd and pulled her forward.

I said, 'It's hard to tell what's what, isn't it? Everything is the same bloodish colour.' Angharad herself was looking a bit grey.

The best part was when Mrs Mac let me stick my finger through the aorta. There was something quite amazing about my pinkie being where blood has pumped. Mrs Mac said, 'It's nice to see you so enthusiastic, Faith.'

I said, 'Well maybe if you brought body parts into the classroom every lesson there'd be less snoozing in the back row.'

I haven't even got to the best part yet. We all shuffled back to our seats and Mrs Mac started tidying up. She was carrying the remains of the heart on this tray thing to the back of the class where the prep room is and telling us about the heart strings. She was so busy she didn't notice that she was holding the tray at an angle, which meant blood was trickling off the back corner, leaving a delightful red-brown trail on the floor. We were all transfixed.

Then she stopped and shifted the tray on to one hand, up high like a waiter, so she could pull up her bra strap with the other hand. (I wish teachers wouldn't draw attention to their underwear. It makes you start to think about what's inside the underwear. And no one wants that.) Now the blood was dripping into a lovely puddle. Angharad was absolutely horrified. It took her two attempts to squeak out, 'Mrs Macready!'

Mrs Mac spun round to see what she wanted and *flicked pig's blood right across Angharad's face*. Angharad swayed forward and then fell off her stool in a dead faint.

Absolutely brilliant.

To be honest, if I died now, at least I'd know that I've seen something truly special.

TUESDAY 4TH OCTOBER

A truly monstrous injustice has been heaped upon me by the Priestess of the Heaping Shovel, old Ramsbottom herself.

Let me start from the beginning.

Yesterday when Angharad came round from her fainting fit, she had a little shriek and then started trying to claw her own face off.

I said, 'Bit of spit on a tissue would probably be more effective, Ang.' But she didn't seem to be listening, so I very kindly and thoughtfully dragged her over to the sink and stuck her head under the tap. Now, you know how powerful those taps are in science labs and how all the water bounces back up and all over the desk? Well, when you stick a head under you get some *serious* splash-back. *But* apart from drenching Megs (bonus!) and making Ang squeal, it was very effective in the blood removal stakes. Overall, Angharad was grateful, if a bit damp, so I had actually been both quick thinking and helpful.

Although not according to Miss Ramsbottom, who it turns out had seen me through the window pulling about a blood-splattered girl and then thrusting her under a tap. So I was called into her office at lunchtime today (when I was supposed to be going on a boy-spotting funfest with Megs) to explain this 'bullying'.

What? What on earth . . .? Number one, does she really think she knows what was going on by looking through a window? And number two, why didn't she sort this out yesterday? When I had time to waste. She probably needed to recharge her batteries by sleeping in a coffin overnight, so she'd be at the height of her evil powers while interrogating me.

I protested my innocence firmly but politely. 'That is the most utterly stupid and ridiculously insane thing I have ever heard, Miss Ramsbottom,' I said, and then explained what had happened. For some reason, Miss Ramsbottom didn't seem to believe me. Why not? Has she met Mrs Mac? If you put teenagers in a lab with pig corpses and a mad Scottish woman, anything could happen. So, Ramsbottom sent for Mrs Mac to come and tell her side of it. Meanwhile my lunchtime was slipping away. I was sure Megs wouldn't go without me, but I needed to speed things up so I said, 'Mrs Macready is probably eating her lunch. Why don't I come back and sort this out later? Two thirty is good for me, I've got French then.'

'You'll wait, Faith.'

'The thing about Mrs Macready is that her knife skills aren't that hot. We could be waiting a long—'

'Faith, you're in enough trouble without making remarks about your teacher's table manners.'

After what felt like forever, Mrs Mac came in and tried to set Miss Ramsbottom straight. It took a long time. It was almost as if Ramsbottom didn't *want* to believe that I am not at the bottom of everything bad that ever happens in the world ever. When Ramsbottom finally let me go (without so much as an apology or large compensation cheque) it was only five minutes to the bell.

I caught up with Megs outside English. 'Stupid Ramsbottom wouldn't let me go. Sorry we missed town. Shall we go tomorrow?'

'Erm . . .'

'Because I know you won't have gone without me, Megs. All through my ordeal with that woman the one thing that kept me going was the idea that my Megs would never abandon me, wouldn't dream of having fun while I was suffering . . .' I caught sight of her face. 'You went without me, didn't you?'

'I thought that you'd want me to.'

'Why would I want you to? Why would I want anyone to be having a nicer time than I am?'

'Well, you are brave and giving, Faith. I was sort of imagining you like one of those soldiers that gets shot and says, "Forget me. Go on without me. Save yourself." That sort of thing.'

'Just for the record, Megs, if I do die in battle, then you are *not* to forget about me. In fact, I would like to be preserved and have each hand sewn to a foot to create straps, so you can carry me about like a rucksack for the rest of your days to remind you of how much you miss me.'

67

Turns out they had a great time in town. There were loads of Year Ten and Elevens from our school and the boys' school hanging around outside the chip shop. Ethan and Cameron were there too and something staggering happened. Cameron asked Megs to swap numbers! I could kill Miss Ramsbottom. Look what I have missed out on.

Megs wasn't suitably apologetic, she just said, 'I thought you'd hang out with your other friend instead.'

This is getting ridiculous; I know Lily is a bit odd, but Megs never had a problem with her before. Maybe they just need to spend more time together.

WEDNESDAY 5TH OCTOBER

Megs is driving me mad. It's all very well swapping numbers with a boy, but what happens next? I think Megs thought they'd be chatting away all last night, but Cameron hasn't rung. Not so much as a text. Not even a smiley. I had to listen to Megs squeaking on about this all through lunch. I was incredibly patient and only hit her over the head twice.

I said, 'Megs, here is a crazy notion. Why don't you ring him?'

'Don't be ridiculous. Just because he has given me his number it doesn't mean I can just go ringing him!'

'I think that might be exactly what it means. You've clearly lost your mind, Megs. I'm just going to move these chocolate fingers out of your way, so you can't do yourself an injury. Don't worry; they'll be safe in my mouth.'

At that moment her mobile went off and she jumped about three metres in the air. She was all fingers and thumbs and could hardly press the buttons.

I said, 'And how is your mum?'

'It's him. Oh my goodness.'

'What does it say?'

She held out her phone. **How R U?**

She said, 'What do you think he means?'

That was just the beginning of her dribbling. Fortunately Megs's mum had packed her a variety of chocolaty treats for her lunch so I let her bang on while I munched.

We spent the whole of Maths on her reply. In the end she wrote, **Good. You?**

I can only hope that I never have to help her write a letter.

THURSDAY 6TH OCTOBER

I woke up this morning feeling a bit off-colour. I was so weak that I was only able to consume two bowls of Coco Pops, a sherbet Dib Dab and a packet of prawn cocktail crisps before school.

I said to Killer Bill in PE, 'Don't expect my usual athleticism, Miss Williams. I am suffering from malnutrition. If you could rustle me up a biscuit or three I might muster the energy for a game of dominoes. Otherwise you should just abandon me in this lonely warm changing room and all go and enjoy yourselves on the hockey field.'

She said, 'How nice of you to volunteer to go in goal, Faith.'

She'd better hope that the day I learn to aim that stupid hockey ball is the day she's wearing her gum shield.

FRIDAY 7TH OCTOBER

Hee hee. I played my trick on Ethan today at rehearsal. It was actually quite hard to think of a prank. Normally I am good at this, but then normally I am trying to upset a teacher. I don't want to upset Ethan, I want him to think that I am a comedy genius (and love goddess) which rules out anything that causes ruined clothes and/or hair loss. Which doesn't leave much.

What I came up with was this: the chairs in the hall are bright orange plastic, so if you place one of those luminous orange Post-it notes on them it's barely visible. This is how Ethan ended up with an orange heart-shaped Post-it on each bottom cheek reading *I love my bum*.

That would have been funny all by itself, but as I was preparing things Westy came bounding up and said, 'What's so funny, Faith?'

When he had finished wetting himself (truly, he said, 'That is so brilliant a tiny bit of pee has come out,' – he is gross) he had the genius idea of calling Ethan down to the front so that everyone would get to see my handiwork.

So, Ethan and the rest of them came in. Cameron sat next to Megs and Elliot almost plonked himself down on the 'special chair', but I managed to shove him out the way. When Ethan sat down Angharad nearly gave the game away by getting the giggles, but then Westy stood at the front of the hall and called Ethan over. Just at that moment Mr M came in and told us all to settle down, so in the almost-silence Ethan walked up the aisle towards Westy, giving everyone a perfect view of his orange-hearted behind. People started laughing and whistling.

Ethan looked back over his shoulder all confused and when he got to the front Westy gave him a note from me which said, *Nice bum!* Ethan looked at his own backside and then shook his head while the rest of the hall were cracking up. Then Ethan said, 'Mr Millet, Faith has got some costume suggestions for the boys.' And turned round and waggled his bottom. Which was quite funny. He can take a joke. I like that in a boy.

Then there was the dull part of rehearsal, i.e. all that singing nonsense. To stop myself suffering brain damage through boredom, I hid Angharad's music, which sent her into a right old panic. (I don't know why, she could always just make it up as she goes along, like I do. I find one note is much the same as another.) Anyway, she had to share Elliot's music, which meant we all got to enjoy Elliot attempting to turn pages over without brushing Angharad's arm. It was very touching and I was almost moved to tears when he said tenderly to her, 'It's quite fast that one, isn't it?' and she giggled and said, 'Yes.'

But my wedding planning was interrupted by Westy saying, 'You know those trees?'

'Not to copy French homework from, but I've chatted to a few.'

'I mean, you know those tiny trees that they breed. Bonsai?'

I knew I'd regret it later, but I said, 'Yeah.'

'Do you think their children would be like that?' He nodded at Ang and Elliot.

'Do I think their children would be tiny trees? Steady on, Westy. Ang's a bit squeamish about Biology in general; I think if she gave birth to a shrub it would finish her off. No amount of sticking her head under the tap would bring her back from that one.'

'Ah.' He nodded his head, like I'd really cleared things up for him.

I didn't have time to try to explain further because fit Finn appeared from nowhere and said to Megs, 'Did you put those stickers on his bum?'

Megs opened her eyes really wide and tossed her hair across her face. Before she had one of his eyes out, I helpfully elbowed her out of the way and said, 'That was me.'

He said, 'Cool,' and nodded to himself. 'Pretty cool.'

I laughed in an infectious way, but he was already ambling off.

Angharad said, 'I'm not sure that Finn entirely understood the more subtle nuances of that practical joke.'

Westy said, 'Yeah.'

Ang and I turned to stare at him.

'I'm just saying . . . he's an idiot.'

Then it was time for a bit more singing. At the end something really amazing happened. Someone Cameron is on a football team with called Ryan is having a party tomorrow and asked Cameron if he wanted to come and Cam asked if he could bring along some girls too (that's us!).

I said, 'Does Ryan mind? Can we come?'

'Are you kidding me? He was like, "Yes!" And then all, "Yeah, that's cool, whatever."'

So we're all going to a proper party, with boys, at someone's house, while their parents are out. I feel so grown up and mature and sophisticated that I could do a roly-poly.

LATER

So I did. Then I added a spin, a star jump and backwards roll. I was having a go at a handspring when I ran out of bedroom space and crashed into Dad on the landing. While he was taking my foot out of his armpit (I know, I will need to triple wash my poor toes before the party) I said, 'Can I go to a party?'

'Will there be boys?'

'Yes.'

'Then no.'

'I don't need a lift. Megs's mum is going to take us.'

'Oh, all right then. Don't be late.'

I felt it best that we didn't get into a discussion on the meaning of 'late'. I think Mum's late might be later than Dad's late. I'll ask her.

SATURDAY 8TH OCTOBER

Megs rang me this morning to discuss the party.

'I said can your mum give Lily and Angharad a lift too?'

There was a bit of a pause. 'We don't have to go everywhere with them, you know,' she said.

'If you'd rather that we toddled into a party where we'll know almost no one with just the two of us looking like sad, lonely, old ladies, who probably live together and fight over who is going to feed the cats, that's fine. I just thought arriving as a pack of stylish young women would suggest that we were popular and fun. But you know me, Megs; I don't want to push you into anything.'

Megs made some nose breathing noises. 'Oh, all right. I'll ask my mum. Now listen, what are we going to wear?'

I said, 'Unless you've got something with four armholes, I think that actually sharing the same outfit might be a bit restrictive.'

'Well, I can't go in jeans if you're wearing a ball gown.'

'I lent my ball gown to my Uncle Rob. Haven't heard from him since he changed his name to Rebecca.'

'Come on, Faith.'

'All right, all right. We can't get too dressed up because we'll look like we're trying too hard. But we don't want to dress down because then we'll blend into the background . . .'

'And no one wants that.'

'Exactly, no one wants that. So, I think the answer is obvious: miniskirts.'

'Faith, that's your answer to everything.'

'And it's a good one. I have no idea why Mrs Mac didn't accept it as an answer to the question, "What do the female of the species do to attract males?"'

'We were talking about insects.'

'I cannot be expected to listen to every detail of Mrs Mac's babbling. The point is that miniskirts fit in anywhere. Including a reasonably-sized handbag.'

'Let me ask you something. What would you wear to meet the queen?'

'A miniskirt. Plenty of leg freedom for curtsying.'

'What about a mountain trek?'

'A waterproof miniskirt. With pockets.'

'A funeral?'

'Black miniskirt.'

'I'd better start exfoliating my knees.'

She should probably shave her toes too, but I didn't mention that.

BIT LATER

It's all very well being sure about the miniskirt thing, but which miniskirt? In order to be sure I will need to try them all on. With a selection of tops. And accessories.

LATER

It's taken two and a half hours but I'm certain that the denim is the way to go.

IF-I-DON'T-HURRY-UP-I'LL-BE-LATE-FOR-THE-PARTY LATER

Or maybe the black one?

THIS-WILL-HAVE-TO-DO LATER

Definitely denim. It gives me the casual air of jeans but the *ooh la la* of my legs.

SUNDAY 9TH OCTOBER

Last night was brilliant. Best. Party. Ever. Well, mostly. It didn't start well. You see, when a boy says, 'I'll send you the directions to the party,' you might expect to get some directions to the party, but that would mean that you have forgotten the golden rule: BOYS ARE DIFFERENT. A girl would provide you with step-by-step instructions from the town centre, mentioning helpful landmarks like Topshop and the massive house where that newsreader lives. A boy sends a road name. And nothing else. No house number, no cryptic clues, not even coordinates.

I didn't know any of this until Megs's mum had dropped off me, Megs, Lily and Angharad on one of those new estates on the edge of town where all the houses look the same, except they're each a tiny bit different. It's like being forced to play spot the difference the whole time.

I pulled my skirt down and my wonderbra up

71

and asked Megs what number Buller Close we wanted.

'Cameron didn't exactly say,' she said.

'What?'

'It doesn't matter. We'll just walk down the road and listen for music.'

Lily wasn't impressed. 'I'm not wearing walking shoes. I'm wearing looking-lovely-on-the-end-of-my-legs-while-I-recline-gracefully shoes.'

'At least I got us invited to a party,' Megs snapped back.

You'd think a teenage party would be easy to spot in a quiet cul-de-sac, but the place was dead. We shuffled down the road holding up Lily and trying to casually peer in people's windows. Then a pack of nine-year-old boys came around the corner on their bikes.

Lily hissed, 'Stop. I can't walk when people are watching.'

The little twerps were riding in circles and staring at us. I propped Lily against a handy lamppost. I was starting to get annoyed.

'Megs, why don't you just text Cameron?' I said.

'I can't just text him! Not just out of the blue like that. What would I say?'

'How about, where the hell are you?'

The snot-rags erupted in laughter.

Lily said, 'They're laughing at my shoes.'

The biggest bratling shouted, 'BOOBS!'

'I don't think it's your shoes he's looking at, Lily.'

'Oh gross, we're being perved on by a preschooler.'

Fortunately, at that point Megs saw Zoe and Becky getting out of a car over the road. Turns out the party was in Buller Court, not Buller Close. So off we slinked.

Also, the interesting thing about a row of pervy little boys on bikes is that if you push the first one over then the rest of them go down like dominoes.

I'm just saying.

LATER

Anyway, when we finally got inside, the first thing I spotted was Icky having a 'water fight' with Dan and about seven hundred and thirteen other boys. Mostly, they were splashing at her white tea towel of a dress and watching it turn see-through while she squealed. She is such a wonderful ambassador for girlkind.

We shuffled into the sitting room, which was crammed with people. I recognised a few girls from school. Some of the boys were staring at us so I guided the girls into a corner.

Lily was still whining, 'Faith, I need a chair. I really need a chair. My feet are killing me. How am I supposed to recline gracefully without a chair?'

I said, 'Lily, all I can offer you is a pot plant. Failing that, Angharad isn't a bad height for perching.'

Angharad was gazing about like a little girl at Christmas. She was wearing a blouse. I kid you not, a full-on floral, puff-sleeved blouse and a knee-length pale blue skirt. I whispered to Megs, 'I sent her a text saying we were wearing miniskirts, why is she wearing that?'

'I think that is a miniskirt.'

I'll never complain about being short again.

Then Ethan and Cameron arrived, followed quickly by Westy and another boy who was almost as wide and as high as he is.

Westy bellowed, 'FAITH! How you doing?'

I was oddly pleased to see him. He's like a gigantic scruffy dog. So I shouted, 'All right. How are you, Westy?'

'Not bad. Got this boil under my arm . . .' Then his huge mate tried to lift up his shirt to have a look. *Ewww*. Westy threw him to the floor and they started hitting each other.

Ethan said, 'It's nice that they're comfortable enough in their manhood to roll around on top of each other, isn't it?'

I said, 'Seems a bit sad to me that a boy has to have his skull fractured to get a cuddle.'

Cam said, 'I can get a cuddle. Megan will give

me a cuddle, won't you?' And he put his arm around Megs, while she tried to look like boys hug her all the time.

Westy scrambled up from the floor. 'Is this a group hug?' Then he flung his arms around me and lifted me off the ground. Man, he's strong. So Megs was getting cosy with Cameron and I was getting crushed by the bear boy. I hope boils aren't catching.

Later on, I ended up chatting to Ethan in the hallway. I asked him if he was on the football team with Cameron.

He said, 'Despite my godlike figure, I'm not. I tend only to run when there's something in it for me. You know, like not being mugged.'

I agreed, 'The only time I've run this year was when my form tutor started flashing everyone's Year Seven photos up on the whiteboard. I had to sprint to throw myself in front of the board so that no one's eyes would bleed from looking at a photo of me with a pineapple ponytail.'

He was staring at me.

'It was my mum's idea,' I explained.

'I've only got a limited understanding of the science of girls' hair. Does a "pineapple ponytail" mean you had fruit on your head?'

'No. Then at least I would have had a snack. It just means I looked stupid.'

He waggled his eyebrows at me. 'I don't know if you realise it, but you're doing that now. Do you want me to throw myself over you to stop people's eyes from bleeding?'

'Ha ha.'

It wasn't the witty answer I was hoping would pop out of my mouth, but I felt a bit odd when Ethan was talking about throwing himself on me. What does that mean?

Then I started to tell Ethan about Angharad and the pig's heart incident. He was laughing a lot and I was enjoying myself when suddenly Icky *bleeping* Blundell appeared, wearing what looked like a wet hanky (seriously, her nipples could have had someone's eyes out if she'd been tall enough, as it is there's fairly nasty nick on my knee that I'm holding her responsible for), and she said, 'Oooh, Ethan (pout, pout), there you are (saucy twinkle), I've been looking for you everywhere (bottom wiggle). We need you to play us that song.' *And he went off with her.*

Well! Up until this point I was thinking that Ethan wasn't completely stupid, but clearly I was wrong. Anyone who follows any kind of instruction from Icky is obviously an idiot. They went to the garden where a load of Radcliffe boys were seeing who could make a guitar sound the most awful. It appears Ethan is quite good at playing the guitar.

(How come Icky knew he played the guitar when I didn't?) Not that I watched them. I had far too much pride. Actually, I couldn't face weaving through the snogging couples in the kitchen, so I sent Angharad instead, as she's pretty useful for spying jobs since she's nearly small enough to fit through a keyhole.

I was starting to think about ringing Dad and asking him what was the meaning of allowing me to stay out this late, and oughtn't he to pick me up right now and say something finishing in 'young lady', when Finn walked in. I didn't think he could look any more astonishing than he does in his school uniform, but he did. He was wearing jeans and a T-shirt like most of the boys there, but somehow his T-shirt made you think about how lovely his arms are and his jeans made me think about his legs, and when I looked at his face I couldn't think about anything because there was the sound of singing in my head.

And then he was gone. I wandered through to the living room, but Megs had disappeared with Cameron and I couldn't see anyone I knew. I flipped through the DVD collection pretending to be really interested in all the small print on the back, but still nobody came to talk to me. I squeezed through the crowds to look for the rest of the girls. The kitchen had cleared of snoggers and

Zoe and Angharad were there comparing eyebrows in Zoe's compact.

Ang said, 'I might just shave mine off. Do you think it would make me look more interesting, Faith?'

'Maybe you could try hair glitter first.'

I could see Icky and some St Mildred's girls in designer jeans had formed a ring around Ethan and the other music types in the garden. I turned my back on them. I was starving. Is it polite to poke through someone you don't know's fridge? Probably not, but maybe these people should have raised their son to take better care of his guests. So I started fixing myself a little snack. Ang and Zoe squeaked about how rude I was – like anyone was going to miss a couple of slices of bread and a bit of squeezy cheese – and I could hear Icky slurping and giggling outside. *Cow*. I slammed my hand down on the cheese tube and – oh my – a glob of cheese shot out, through the air and landed on the chest of someone who'd just walked into the kitchen.

It was Finn.

I went bright purple and tried to climb inside the cheese tube. I thought he would say something really cutting, but he just said, 'Whoa! Steady.'

How nice is that? I kept saying sorry, and Ang and Zoe were stood there with their mouths open.

Then Finn actually lifted up his T-shirt and licked the cheese off. I know it's weird but that made me really like him. He might look like a god, but he licks cheese like a boy. He said, 'I prefer it with a cracker. T-shirt fluff just isn't as crunchy.'

We all laughed. Zoe laughed so hard she snorted.

He said, 'Good sandwich.'

Which I took to mean that he was helplessly attracted to me.

'You go to Westfield, don't you?'

I said, 'Yes.' Which didn't seem like enough of an answer, so I added, 'I do.' Which are two words you should not say in any boy's presence. Ever. But he didn't seem to notice.

So we had an actual conversation. Finn and me (and Ang and Zoe, but I think Finn mostly spoke to me). He's nice. He told us about being on the football team with Ryan and I found out that we both like a variety of cheese products. Anyway, we must have talked for at least ten whole minutes when Megs came to tell me that it was time to go.

It was a good party.

I don't think I ever put the squeezy cheese back in the fridge.

MONDAY 10TH OCTOBER

I've finally got to the bottom of Megs's anti-Lily business.

At breaktime I was chatting to Lily when Megs came stropping over. She got right in Lily's face and said, 'What is your problem?'

Lily looked even more confused than usual.

'Don't give me that innocent idiot look. I can see right through you.'

'Er, Megs,' I said, 'I hate to stop you because all the people who are staring at you are obviously enjoying the show, but what the hell are you going on about?'

'I saw her! I saw her chatting up Cameron. Everyone knows that I like Cameron and that we're practically . . . well, maybe not practically . . . but almost—'

'Again, Megan, *what are you talking about?*'

'She's trying to steal my boyfriend! My nearly boyfriend! First she steals my best friend and now she's going after Cameron.'

And, having finished demonstrating just how utterly crazy she is, Megs ran off to the toilets.

So all this time Megs has been jealous of Lily.

How adorable is that?

Adorable, but also insane and quite annoying. I went after Megs and shouted under the locked toilet door. 'I love you best! No one can ever take me away from you! I will always love and respect you for the wonderful, intelligent young woman you are. Now come on out, you stupid idiot.'

She shuffled out the door blubbing and I was forced to hug her.

'Do you really hate Lily?' I asked.

Megs wiped her nose on my sleeve. 'A bit. I'm not happy about her chatting up Cameron.'

'I'm not sure that Lily knows how to chat anyone up. Most of her chatting is about her favourite hats and things she's learnt from reading cereal packets. I don't think that's what boys go for.'

Megs didn't seem entirely convinced.

'What about Angharad? Do you hate her too?'

'I tried, but I couldn't.'

I could understand that, hating Ang would be like hating a teddy bear.

'Anyway the thing is that you've been friends with Lily for a really long time. You've known her since primary school,' Megs sniffed.

'Yes, and I've known my granny since I was born, that doesn't make her my bestie. You're my best friend, Megan, and you always will be.'

We gave each other super-soppy smiles.

And then I put her in a headlock just to reinforce my point.

TUESDAY 11TH OCTOBER

Angharad mouse-scuttled up to Megs this morning and tapped her on the shoulder. Megs turned round and Ang cringed backwards.

'Please don't shout at me,' she said in a rush, 'but I wanted you to know that Lily isn't trying to steal Cameron. I was there when they were talking and Lily only said that you're nice, well, she said something about talking horses as well, but I didn't really understand that part and I don't think Cameron did either. But honestly, Cameron said, "You're Megan's friend, aren't you?" and Lily just said how cool you are. I'm not making it up.' She was gasping for breath when she finished. Megs looked at me. We both knew that she was telling the truth.

Megs went a bit pale and said, 'Thank you for telling me, Angharad.' Then she slumped against the wall. 'Oh Faith, I can't believe how mean and horrible I've been to Lily!'

'I know. You've been awful. First you were sniffy with her, then you came right out and accused her of stealing your friend and now—'

'Stop it! I know what I've done. What am I going to do to make it better?'

What she did was to buy her own body weight in sweeties and present them to Lily and say, 'I am very, very sorry. I will never be a jealous cow again.'

And Lily said, 'That's OK.' Which I thought was extremely nice and understanding of her.

We all met up at lunchtime, but things were

still a bit uncomfortable. I thought that some sort of activity might be less painful than chatting, but being a model student has seriously limited the pastimes that are open to me. However, we all know that there's nothing more wholesome than exercise. Also, sport is great for teamwork, isn't it? I thought it might be good for building bridges between Megs and Lily. So I got those two plus Angharad, Zoe and Becky enjoying the healthy and stimulating activity of Sumo wrestling.

The two competitors put on everyone else's coats and then tried to bump each other out of the circle I'd drawn. It was very exciting and it definitely cheered everybody up, plus – most importantly – I am brilliant at it.

I said to the girls, 'I think I may have discovered the sport for me.'

Angharad said, 'I thought you hated sport.'

'Nonsense. There are a few sports that I prefer not to participate in, but that's only the ones that involve running, sweating, water or balls.'

Megs added, 'Or horses.'

'Or horses,' I agreed. 'Other than that, I have long been searching for the sport I would shine at. I always knew I had sporting potential. I used to be worried that my hidden talent was for pole vaulting and that it would remain hidden forever, but now I know that it's Sumo for me.'

I can hardly believe that it's taken me this long to find an activity that combines my skills for dressing up, overeating and violence.

Miss Ramsbottom was not interested in my Olympic hopes. She just flounced past us on the netball court and said, 'Must you make such a racket, girls?'

After that we played Silent Sumo, which was even funnier.

LATER

Why is Miss Ramsbottom such a misery? Why can't she be more like Mrs Webber? When she saw us Sumo-ing she leant out the window of the staff room and yelled, 'Knock her legs out from underneath her, Angharad!'

WEDNESDAY 12TH OCTOBER

Hilarious. Our dear old headmistress had a tantrum today.

Miss Pee is obsessed with everything being in its proper place: bags on pegs, girls in classrooms, PE skirts around waists instead of being worn as a cape, you know, all that sort of OCD nonsense. She is especially particular about her parking space. Absolutely no one else is allowed to park there. Probably because it's the best parking space in the school grounds. It's protected from both the rain and bright sun by a lovely shady tree and it's the only space right outside the main entrance. The other spaces are a good thirty metres away and, to be fair to old Miss Pee, if she had to walk that far her ancient bones would probably crumble to dust.

Today, it seems she had popped out at lunchtime (I like to imagine that she went to get a Big Mac, but in reality she probably went to WHSmith's to buy some of those metal rulers so she could 'accidentally' slice off a few Year Sevens' fingers with them) and when she came back to school, the window cleaners' van was parked in her spot. I was lucky enough to be strolling by with Megs. Actually, we are banned from hanging out at the front of the school 'making the place look untidy', but we were on our way back from the corner shop – no one should be expected to sit through double French without the comfort of a few sweeties. It's a pretty scary language. Do you know that every single noun is a boy or a girl? That's just making work for yourself. And who decided that a table is masculine? All my granny's tables are covered in doilies.

Anyway, Megs and I were skulking through the bushes when we saw Miss Pee and Mr Freeborn, the school caretaker, having a heated discussion. Miss Pee stamped her foot (yes, it was that serious) and was jabbing at the van and raging about the window cleaners' rudeness in parking in her space. Poor old Mr Freeborn was obviously trying to calm her down, but she growled, 'This is entirely unacceptable.' Her pearls were quivering with rage. 'Move that thing NOW!'

I'm afraid I missed the end of their conversation because Megs pointed out that I was going to miss singing the birthday song in French.

LATER

During French I asked Lily how she was getting on with Megs. She said, 'Fine.' As if she was surprised that I'd asked.

'Aren't you angry about the things she said to you?'

'No, I felt a bit sorry for her really. She was just feeling threatened, wasn't she? I knew that once she knew that you'll always like her best she'd come round.'

I was so staggered by Lily showing such insight into another human being that I could hardly speak. 'So you don't mind? You're not . . . cross or anything?'

'No, I like Megs, she wears great socks.'

I can't say that I've looked at Megs's socks recently, but it was just a relief to hear Lily say something Lilyish again.

I can only hope that all this nonsense is over.

LATERER
Because it would be terrible to have people fighting over me all the time.

LATER STILL
I might describe this whole incident to Granny next time she asks me if I'm popular.

THURSDAY 13TH OCTOBER
Heard today that those naughty window cleaners were actually having a cup of tea and eating doughnuts with the kitchen staff. Apparently, Miss Pee was furious. I am furious too. I have never even *seen* a doughnut at school. Where have they been hiding them all this time? Clearly, down the necks of workmen.

I wonder how Miss Pee explained to the window cleaners the hugeness of their crime. I reckon that it's not just that it's the best parking space, I think that Miss Pee likes to park her big shiny car there so that she can keep looking out the window of her office and saying, 'That's mine, that is.' Old people are so immature.

Everyone was talking about Miss Pee's tantrum. I don't know how so many people knew about it. Megs and I can only have managed to get round to a hundred or so girls before registration.

Anyway, I got a standing ovation in History

when I arrived (a mere six minutes late) and found Limp Lizzie in my favourite seat. I said, 'This is entirely unacceptable,' then I pointed at her and said, 'Mr Freeborn, move that thing NOW!' Ah, how everyone laughed. Even Miss Wood tried so hard not to giggle that she accidentally bit the cap off the board marker she was holding. She ended up with blue ink all round her mouth, but we didn't mention it.

FRIDAY 14TH OCTOBER

Brilliant rehearsal. We got there in time to see Finn stroll in and the first thing he said was, 'Hey ... Faith.'

If I'm being really picky there was quite a long pause between the 'hey' and the 'Faith', but I think that's just the speed that he speaks. It's like he's not quite of this world. Besides, he must meet a lot of girls and he obviously doesn't speak to all of them because once he'd sauntered off to the piano almost every female in the room was hissing at me under their breath.

Megs just said, 'He's a bit sure of himself.'

I said, 'You'd be sure of yourself if you looked like that.'

'If I looked like that I wouldn't be sure at all. I'd wonder why my parents had raised me as a girl when I quite clearly had a boy's body.'

'There's no need to bring your weird gender issues into this.'

She looked at me. 'What do you mean my gender issues?'

'Megs, we all know you enjoyed wearing that beard when we did Macbeth in Year Eight . . . And I haven't forgotten that time you stood up to pee.'

'You've been known to enjoy sporting facial hair yourself and that loo seat looked very unhy—'

'If I promise to give you some proper therapy when you're rich enough to pay me for it, do you think we could go back to talking about Finn?'

'I just don't like people who are too sure of themselves.'

'So you think we should all be insecure together?'

'Well, it's much more friendly.'

I don't think that Finn is too sure of himself. He's just very relaxed. Mellow. He's nice to everyone.

I tried being on the frosty side to Ethan to show him what I thought of him abandoning me at the party to go and spend time with Icky. He didn't even have the manners to notice. So I decided to use subtle questioning to discern his motives for hanging out with her ickiness.

I said, 'Why the hell were you talking to the tiny troll at the party?'

He laughed. 'Vicky is a bit high-pitched, isn't she?'

I, of course, am too well-mannered to criticise other girls, so I just nodded my head. Quite a lot.

'And a bit . . . pushy. I really just wanted a go on that guitar. It's Ryan's dad's Dreadnought.'

It seems not all guitars are the same. I gathered that some are better than others and some are so exciting that they make your eyes go shiny. Ethan was quite sweet and glowy when he started talking about the Battlestar or whatever it's called. I found myself actually listening to him explain the kind of guitar sound he likes best (grainy, apparently). I was thinking about asking him for a lesson when Finn ambled past and gave me a thumbs up.

Ethan saw him and said, 'And what about who you were chatting to at the party? What did you and Beach Bum find to talk about? Hair care?'

Which annoyed me. I didn't know that Ethan had seen me talking to Finn and I didn't think it was fair of him to suggest that it was trivial. I couldn't bear to prove him right by saying we mostly talked about cheese, so I said, 'Just . . . stuff.'

Then there was a bit of a pause and before I could get back to the guitar lesson Mr Millet was making noises at us and I had to start singing and pretending to know what he was talking about. Obviously, I didn't do this very well because a couple of times Lily and Megs started cracking up at my attempts to follow Mr M's nonsense instructions. At least they seem to be getting along a bit better. At the end I wanted to talk to Ethan again, but straight away he started chatting to Lily. I hope he enjoyed his lecture on the history of her shoe collection.

SATURDAY 15TH OCTOBER

This morning I was just settling down for a post-breakfast snooze on the sofa when the doorbell rang.

Mum said, 'That will be Granny.'

This is obviously Mum's new tactic. Previously, when she has heralded Granny's arrival by insisting on house cleaning and the brushing of hair, she has found herself in a strangely empty house by the time Granny arrives, so this time she went for a surprise attack. Both Sam and I sprang towards the window.

Mum said, 'It's locked. Sit down and be polite.'

To be fair to Granny, I've always found that she's not that bothered whether you are polite or not. She tells you off either way.

She came in and said, 'There are my grandchildren, or at least I think they are. I haven't seen them in so long.' Then she took out her hanky and wiped the sofa before she sat down.

I sat back and tried to lose consciousness whilst still nodding and smiling. Talking to Granny is a lot like being lectured by Miss Ramsbottom. Only I don't bother with the smiling for that.

In the end, Granny caught my attention by saying, 'You're a growing girl and I expect you're expensive to keep in clothes.'

I nearly said, *Yes, but the neighbours complain when I go without,* but I thought I could hear the papery rustle of some cash coming my way so I kept quiet. She started fishing about in her shopper bag and I started planning a trip to Topshop.

She pulled out a carrier bag. 'So I've brought you some of my things.'

My mouth fell open. Which Granny seemed to take as a sign of gratitude. 'That's all right; I needed some new clothes for my mini-break with Peter anyway. And you may as well have these things now. It will all be yours when I'm dead.'

Which is crafty when you think about it. She's giving me an incentive to keep her alive.

LATER

When Granny had left, I said to Mum, 'Make sure you keep those windows locked tonight, otherwise she might just fly right back in.'

Mum said, 'Faith, I won't have you making your granny sound like a witch. It isn't fair.' She fished out the sweet wrappers Granny had stuffed down the side of the sofa. 'All the witches I've known have been very sweet ladies.'

Which just goes to show. Mum might be an old hippy, but we can all see where I get my sharp tongue from.

I took my bag of treats from Granny upstairs, along with Sam's football gloves which I put on for protection before pulling out the charming selection of items she'd given me: one turquoise polyester blouse with shoulder pads and 'jewel' buttons, one vest-style top with a parrot embroidered on it *in sequins* and one pointy black bra. The size on the label of the bra had faded away, but when Sam wandered in and saw me holding it up in horror he said, 'Can I have that so I can make a couple of wizard hats?'

I didn't give it to him, because it goes against my nature to say yes to anything he asks, but now I realise I want it myself. Ethan's going to get a nasty surprise.

SUNDAY 16TH OCTOBER

Yesterday afternoon I took Granny's cast-offs (except the bra) to a charity shop. There was a girl manning the till who, if you ignored the pierced nose and scary eye makeup, looked like she was about eight years old.

I went up to her and said, 'Can I swap these for something nice?'

She sniffed. 'We haven't got anything nice, but you can have a look at our rubbish.'

I thought that was a bit judgemental coming from a small girl in high heels and a gold crop top, but it turns out she was right. There was nothing worth having in the whole shop.

In the end I found three My Pretty Ponies, like the ones I had when I was little, and they gave me a good idea. The little girl made me pay for them (apparently it's not a swapping situation and you're supposed to just give away your stuff to these places – no wonder they're full of junk). I watched her to make sure she put the money in the till. I didn't want her spending my cash on another piercing.

MONDAY 17TH OCTOBER

Miss Pee has had 'Headmistress' painted on her parking space in big white letters! I've got to say that if she wants to stop people parking there, a traffic cone might be more effective.

It's also going to be quite hard for me to walk past the word 'Headmistress' every day and resist the urge to cross out 'mistress' and write 'case'.

Anyway, while Megs and I were admiring Miss Pee's parking space craziness, a lady in a suit came up to us. But I couldn't tell you what colour the suit was because I was entirely distracted by the massive chain around her neck. You know, like a mayor or a rapper. She almost fell over Megs, who had got down on her hands and knees to take a picture with her phone of a dead bird that we thought Miss Pee had probably sacrificed to the parking space gods. The woman skipped backwards sharpish, like she thought Megs might bite.

I said, 'Don't worry, she won't hurt you. Since we put the chip in her head, she's done a lot less savaging.'

The woman smiled at me. Sometimes I wonder if people are actually listening to what I say.

She said, 'I do hope you young ladies can help me. I've come to present some certificates in this afternoon's assembly. Do you think you could show me the way to reception?'

It was almost time for the end-of-lunch bell to ring, but I thought that showing visitors about was probably a legitimate excuse for being late for registration, so I agreed that Megs and I would show her the way.

As we strolled along, Angharad flew past us, red in the face and gasping. Obviously, she was terrified of missing those vital first few minutes of registration when people are finishing their lunch and the teacher is making up her next lesson.

The lady said, 'Gosh, someone's in a hurry!' But Angharad was going too fast to answer.

I said, 'She doesn't talk much outside of lessons. She's exhausted, poor little thing. She's only nine you know, but the head says she must be milked for GCSE results.'

The woman gave me a bit of a stare, but her friendly-friendly smile stayed plastered to her face.

As we were coming down the main corridor I spotted Ramsbottom coming out of her office. I yanked the woman and Megs round the corner to reception at breakneck speed.

The lady said, 'What on earth—?'

I said, 'It's the High Commander. We're not allowed to look upon her face.'

I elbowed Megs in the ribs and she managed to squeeze out a few tears and whine, 'I don't want to go back to the basement.' She grabbed the woman by the arm for effect. 'Please don't let her take me back to the basement.'

We were stood at reception by this point. The woman switched off her smiley face and she snapped at me, 'That's a silly way to talk, isn't it? What's your name, young lady?'

And I said, 'Victoria Blundell.'

LATER

And, you know, we may not have taken the quickest route, but round the back of the smokers' bike-shed and past the gap in the fence where girls crawl out to meet Radcliffe boys is definitely one way to reception.

I'm just saying.

TUESDAY 18TH OCTOBER

It's racism, that's what it is. It's a slur on my ginger ancestry. That bechained woman asked for a name and I gave her one, but no, she has to go dragging my hair into this. And *apparently* I am the only redhead in the school, because as soon as Miss Ramsbottom heard the 'g' word she was convinced that I am to blame for the 'appalling rudeness' to a 'distinguished guest'. Please. I tried to explain that if we were nice to a woman like that she'd only come back again, but Ramsbottom wasn't listening. Good thing old chain lady doesn't seem to have shared exactly what I said; only that she didn't think much of my 'tone'.

Even so, I have been banned from performing in the concert with the choir. Megs, on the other hand, has simply been warned not to be so 'easily led'. Easily led? If she were easy to lead then I wouldn't have to shout at her so much. It's so unfair. The fact that Megs looks a bit dim always works in her favour. Whereas I am so wickedly good-looking that people always assume I'm up to mischief. Ramsbottom says I'm not fit to represent the school at the concert. I explained that she was getting it all wrong.

I said, politely but firmly, 'I don't even want to represent the poxy school! I just want to spend time with boys.'

But it seems that Miss Ramsbottom has no wish to support teenage girls with their hopes and dreams. I am still banned from the choir.

LATER

Which is not the way I had imagined things at all. I thought that I would leave the choir due to creative differences and release a solo album before getting a part in *EastEnders*.

Life is strange.

WEDNESDAY 19TH OCTOBER

Unbelievable. First thing this morning Megs started having a go at me for breaking my promise to behave myself. I pointed out that she forced me into that promise and also that she joined in with being rude to the chain lady. Megs was opening and shutting her mouth like a goldfish, about to try and make it all my fault again, when Lily chimed in saying, 'Yeah, but Faith, when you start doing one of your things you just sort of sweep people along with it and it's quite hard to say "no".'

'What do you mean by that?'

'Well, you know, you start giving us looks or sticking your sharpest body parts in our softest body parts until we do what you want us to do.'

I was outraged but Megs said, 'Exactly.' And even little Ang was nodding her head a bit.

Well. There you go. I wanted them all to get on and now they are. They're getting on so well that they're ganging up on me.

LATER

I was so cross that I ignored Megs for the whole of Chemistry. Which meant that for once I heard every slowly-drawn-out word that Mr Hampton said. I won't be doing that again in a hurry. By the time Megs started pushing notes written on filter paper begging forgiveness in my direction I was ready to forgive her just to get out of the trance that Mr Hampton's droning was sending me into. Anyway, when you think about it, what Megs, Lily and Angharad are really saying is that I am so charismatic and persuasive that they will do anything I ask them to.

I don't have a problem with that.

THURSDAY 20TH OCTOBER

Miss Ramsbottom has no idea what an inconvenience she is to me. Now I will have to think of an alternative location for my trick on Ethan. She's a terrible teacher. When people decide that they don't want a proper career and go to teaching school instead, surely the first thing they learn is that they should nurture their students? Ramsbottom probably wasn't listening. I bet she was sat at the back with an ouija board consulting the dark forces.

FRIDAY 21ST OCTOBER

Thank goodness I have made it up with Megs; I would have hated to have missed her lengthy rambling about Cameron today. I don't even need to add in brackets that I am being sarcastic because it is obvious.

Unfortunately it was not obvious to Megs when I said, 'Do go on, Megs, I am so interested,' after ten minutes of her chatter.

Because she just went on. And on.

Ever since Cameron gave her that hug, plus some hand squeezing and a little bit of tickling, she can talk of nothing else.

I said, 'I'm not sure that it is anything to get excited about. If you think about it, I give you all that and more on a daily basis.'

'That's because you love me so much.'

'Nonsense. Most of the times that I pat you it's because I've just washed my hands and there aren't any paper towels left.'

'Do you think that Cameron might want to kiss me?'

'Yes.'

'Because I know that he was chatting to that Lauren girl at the party but do you think . . .'

'Yes.'

'Don't just be negative, try to see it from all angles—'

'YES! MEGAN, THAT BOY LIKES YOU.'

'Do you really think so?'

'He looks at you soppily. He's always trying to sit next to you. And even when you gave him an electric shock at the party from all that Lycra you were wearing he still wanted to "arm wrestle" you.'

'So what makes you think that he likes me?'

At this point I thought I'd rest my voice, so I just let her babble on and occasionally held up a little flash card I'd made that said *He lurves you*.

I endured fifty minutes of Megs dribbling about Cameron in one ear and Mr Hampton monotoning about atoms in the other. It's fortunate that I was able to browse the latest New Look range on Zoe's BlackBerry or I may have been forced to read my Chemistry textbook in order to remain conscious.

Eventually Megs said, 'I think I just need to stop

obsessing about Cameron and go with the flow.' She let out this long breath. 'So . . . do you think he'll ask me out?'

'He might and he might not. We've only got twelve precious hours left in this day, so we should probably devote them to agonising over that question, but before we do I was just wondering – how is that not obsessing working out for you?'

And then I made a little tent out of my Chemistry book and had a nap.

LATER

Everyone else went off to have fun and snogs at the rehearsal, so I went to wait for them in the library. Miss Ramsbottom hasn't banned me from the library. In fact she probably thinks I don't even know where the library is, whereas, the truth is I found it today all by myself.

Using only the map Megs had drawn me.

I may have also recruited a Year Seven to help pull me up the three flights of stairs.

No wonder the place was deserted. If you were fit enough to get there you may as well go to extra sports practice. At least there you get to hit people with sticks and balls and things.

Books are less aerodynamic and therefore, I have discovered, much harder to throw.

I'm just saying.

LATERER

When they eventually dribbled out of the hall, Megs did not seem keen on my full body hug, although Westy did say, 'Can I have one of those?'

They all stood about shuffling a bit with Cameron saying, 'What are you doing now?' and Megs giggling. Well, you can waste time like that if you've already had an hour and a half of male company, but I wanted to get on with things.

I said, 'She's going to the juice bar and so are you lot.'

Westy said, 'I love it when you get strict, Faith.'

LATER STILL

When we got to Juicy Lucy's half of the choir were already there, including Icky. Ethan left his bag under the table while he went to get a Coke, so I reached underneath and managed to stuff Granny's bra in without anyone noticing.

I did take the precaution of saying, 'Vicky, why don't you treat us to one of your table dances?' which meant everyone's eyes were fixed on a different set of underwear while I did the deed. Then I told Westy that I wanted him to get Ethan to open his bag. I suggested that he ask him if he wouldn't mind letting him have a look at his homework because he wanted to check some answers. Just to compare notes and he'd give it straight back. And thanks very much and that sort of thing.

Westy said, 'Give me your Maths book, you idiot.'

Which, to be fair, worked just as well.

Ethan lifted his bag on to the table and opened it up. He stuck in a hand and frowned. Then he pulled out the bra and lifted it up, which was nice because now the whole of the back seating area (i.e. loads of people from both schools) could see Ethan holding up a granny bra at chest level. Excellent.

There was a lot of whooping and whistling. It was particularly nice to see Megs and Lily cackling and clutching at each other. Ethan's neck turned red. I was a bit worried for a moment that he was angry, but then he held the bra up again and said, 'Westy, this is absolutely the last time I am doing your washing.' And he stuffed the bra down the back of Westy's jumper. Lots more whooping.

Perhaps I should go into the entertainment industry. I have brought much joy to many people.

Ethan sat down next to me and said, 'You absolute cow.' But, you know, in a friendly way. 'Just you wait,' he added with a grin, which for some reason made me think about snogging him.

SATURDAY 22ND OCTOBER

Finally it's half-term! A lovely week of no school, no homework and no Miss Ramsbottom. A chance to live my life as nature intended, with fun and boys and regular snacks.

On Tuesday we are meeting the boys in town and on Friday there is the 'disco' in a village hall near where Elliot lives. Megs wasn't keen when she heard it was some churchy type thing.

I said to her in our evening phone chat, 'O little town of Bethlehem, Megs, you cannot let a little thing like God stand between you and a boy. Cameron will be there and that is all that matters.'

'I'm not dancing with a vicar.'

'And the vicar has already said he wants nothing to do with you, so that's all right. Now get round here, I need you to score all my handbags out of ten.'

SUNDAY 23RD OCTOBER

Granny announced she was coming round again today. I said to Dad, 'This is why I said we shouldn't have given her our new address when we moved.'

Dad looked like a rabbit in the headlights, which is what happens when he wants to agree with me, but is afraid that if he does Mum will throw her non-leather vegan shoes at him. It's too much for his tiny mind and everything shuts down, leaving him gawping and wide-eyed.

Sam said, 'Can you keep looking like that, Dad?

Until Granny gets here? Then she can talk about how simple you look instead of me.'

Mum sighed. 'She's never called you simple, Sam.'

'Yes she has. She also said my eyes were too close together and that I have the overbite of a farm labourer.'

'You've got to remember that Granny grew up in a different time.'

I said, 'Yes, in her day you had to get your insults out quick before the dinosaurs ate you.'

LATER

When Granny arrived the first thing she said to me was, 'I expect your hair will get less garish as you get older.' Then she fixed Dad with a dirty look and said, 'She doesn't get it from my side of the family, you know.' She settled herself in the most comfortable chair and told us what's wrong with Tesco.

I did tell Mum that ring-shaped chocolate biscuits were a mistake. It meant that Granny could demolish half a plateful whilst still talking through the hole in the middle and explaining that the man on cold meats isn't as hygienic as he ought to be.

I'd reached a sort of state of semi-consciousness when I heard Mum say, 'I'm sure Faith would love to help.'

I sat bolt upright and said, 'This is a very important year for me at school. I've really only got time for studying. And parties.'

Granny said, 'This is exactly why the old folks need looking after. Young people are so obsessed with their own lives.'

Apparently Granny wants help packing up Christmas boxes for old people. I said I'd think about it and then I leant in for the last biscuit, which completely distracted her; by the time she'd snatched it up and scoffed it down she'd gone back to talking about the number of tattoos on the checkout staff at Tesco.

MONDAY 24TH OCTOBER

I picked up the phone to ring Megs this morning and straight away Dad started whining, 'You spoke to Megan last night! What can possibly have happened since then that is so vital that you need to share it with her immediately?'

'I know that not much goes on inside your head, Father, but many ground-breaking flashes of inspiration have come to me in the last twelve hours. Now if you'll excuse me, I need to impart my wisdom to my best friend.' And in a very dignified fashion I dialled Megs's number and when she answered I said, 'What do you think of luminous nail varnish for the disco?'

Dad pretended to pull his hair out in what I felt was quite a childish way.

TUESDAY 25TH OCTOBER

Went into town today. The high street is much more exciting when it's full of boys. Not much shopping went on (how do boys get clothes? I don't think I have ever seen a boy buying an item of clothing), but there was some good hanging about by the fountain in the shopping centre.

At lunchtime we went to the Sandwich Shop and sat upstairs. I got a banana milkshake and shared some chips with Megs. Not the most nutritious meal, usually I like to include something from the cheese and chocolate food groups too, but it's hard to eat around boys, I'm always worrying about getting something on my chin. We sat at a table with Cameron (next to Megs), Ethan (next to me) and Westy, Elliot, Lily and Angharad.

I should have known that something was up because Westy kept sniggering. But he sniggered every time someone's chair squeaked on the rubber floor and it sounded like a fart, so I'd stopped paying attention to him. Which means I was totally unprepared for trouble when I took a big swig of my milkshake ... and spat it straight back out. It was hot. It was burning hot. My mouth was on fire. I reached for Megs's Coke and that's when I realised everyone was looking at me and laughing their heads off.

And that I had spat my milkshake all over Ethan.

I was almost mortified, but I reckon people who put chillies in other people's (expensive) banana milkshakes deserve to get my banana spit all down their jumper, so I just swapped my milkshake for his juice and said, 'Ethan, let me give you a tip. It's not a very good joke if you're the one who ends up covered in milkshake.'

It was quite funny really. When we said goodbye later he gave me what I like to think of as a particularly affectionate punch because I said, 'You smell like monkey sick.'

WEDNESDAY 26TH OCTOBER

Megs had to go and visit her cousins today and Angharad was busy with her mum, so I thought I'd go to the cinema with Lily. Bearing in mind Megs's recent hysterical jealousy, I thought it best to ring her and show that I was sensitively considering her feelings. I said, 'If I go to the cinema with Loopy Lily will you cry like a baby?'

'It's fine. But you're not allowed to play Popcorn Pants. Some things are sacred.'

On the way to the cinema, out of the bus window, we saw Finn walking a puppy. I tapped on the glass, but he didn't look round.

Lily said, 'I'm not surprised. He's on his own little planet.'

My mouth fell open. The idea that Lily could possibly describe anyone as on their own planet was just unbelievable. 'What do you mean?'

'He's just seems a bit . . .' She started chipping off her nail varnish.

'A bit what?'

'A bit what, what?'

'You said Finn was a bit . . . You didn't finish.'

'He's a bit sketchy, isn't he?'

'He's not sketchy!'

She shrugged, 'He's all right . . .'

'All right? He's gorgeous.'

'I suppose so. But I think he's, you know, bland.'

'Bland?'

'Yeah. He never really says anything. Or does anything.'

'Maybe he's never said anything to you, but I've had loads of conversations with him.'

'What about?'

'Well, there was that time with the cheese spread at the party and he once told me that he doesn't like wearing a tie.'

Lily sniffed. 'You can't get much blander than cheese spread,' she said.

I was getting tired of this conversation, so I decided it was time to use my most sophisticated arguing techniques. I stamped on her foot and said, 'Shut up, you troll, he's nice.'

Lily opened a packet of wine gums and stuffed two in my mouth. She said, 'I know he's nice.'

'What? What are you talking about then?'

'I just don't think you're very well suited to "nice". I always imagined you with more of a "naughty".'

I was a bit freaked out by Lily discussing human nature and stringing together sentences and everything, but I needn't have worried, the next thing she said was, 'Do you think dogs have ambitions?'

LATER

I've been thinking, and a small part of me feels that maybe Lily has made a good point.

Has the world gone crazy?

THURSDAY 27TH OCTOBER

Actually, I've decided that Lily is wrong. This is because a) she usually is and b) we don't really know that much about Finn. I suspect that beneath his angelic good looks lurks a cheeky boy who knows how to be a right monkey (whilst having bouncy hair).

FRIDAY 28TH OCTOBER

Back from the disco. Had a fantastic time. Those religious types really know how to throw a party. I wonder if they do weddings.

Elliot lives in a terrifying village where there are no shops and not even a drive-through McDonald's. I imagine that all the old people who have gone there to die were really pleased to see fifty teenagers arriving this evening. I know the coffin-dodgers always enjoy being surrounded by youth. I once asked Granny what she liked best about me and she said, 'I enjoy seeing your knee joints work smoothly.' She'll be harvesting me for organs soon.

Anyway, I don't think we were too disruptive. Only a bit of cheerful singing and some high-spirited wrestling from the boys. Westy did do a bit of damage by stuffing Elliot in a wheelie bin and running him around over a flowerbed, but if you believed all teenagers were like Westy you wouldn't want to leave the house.

When Megs and I got to the village hall we thought we were the first to arrive. Inside it was just Angharad and Elliot having a jolly old time shoe gazing and asking each other the time and living it up like that. There was also a couple of primary school kids slow-dancing to gangsta rap.

Turned out that all the action was out the back. There was a fieldy bit with some trees and a stream behind the hall and everybody was watching the boys climb trees and then jump out of them. Which was more fun than it sounds. You can get quite a good stare at a boy while he's jumping out of a tree without anyone noticing you're doing it.

After a while I said to Megs, 'Are those bushes moving?'

'It's not the bushes moving. It's the people in them.'

She was right. The shrubbery was crammed with snogging couples.

Later on we saw Icky hogging a whole hedge, but as I said to Megs, 'She needs the room for a turnstile.' Becky said that she definitely saw her snogging both Dan and a friend of Finn's. Although not at the same time. Even Icky's gob isn't that big.

There were also some St Mildred's girls there. I don't know why, but their fantastic good looks and willingness to snog anything in trousers proved quite popular. I can't understand how boys fail to see that they are stuck-up witches.

Fortunately, they didn't get their French-manicured claws into our group of boys. We spent most of the night with Ethan, Cameron, Westy and Elliot and we all had a good laugh.

Ethan was trying to teach me how to hold your fingers for different guitar chords (this involved him touching my hands a bit, which I have to admit I enjoyed), when we were interrupted by a lot of shouting in the middle of the field.

'Hey, Faith, look at me!'

It was Westy hanging upside-down from the top branch of a tree. He was a good five metres up.

I said, 'Get down, you idiot!'

'Yeah, I'm not saying that's a bad idea . . .' He tried to swing up and grab the branch with his hands but he missed. '. . . I'm just not sure I can.'

Then the branch gave this horrible creak.

'Shall I just let go? I mean I'll have my head to break the fall, won't I?'

I turned to Ethan, but he was already halfway up the tree. I've never seen someone climb so fast.

I said, 'Don't panic, Westy. Ethan's going to help you.'

'I'm not panicking. I am sweating though.'

Ethan was crawling towards him. He said, 'Let's hope you're downwind of me then because you really don't want me passing out.'

Ethan got him to work up a bit of swing and then grabbed Westy by the arm and pulled him into a sitting position. They made their way back towards the ground and Westy slid down the last bit of the trunk like a fireman's pole and everyone started cheering.

Why do boys do things that put your heart in your mouth? Like trying to fall out of trees.

Or telling you that you've got nice hands.

SATURDAY 29TH OCTOBER

Sam is being particularly annoying at the moment. He disagrees with everything I say, even when I am saying things which have been scientifically proven. Like, 'You are such a worm, Sam.'

He has definitely been in my bedroom and he has definitely been moving stuff about. Anyway, while I was checking if Sam had been at my secret chocolate stash, I came across the My Pretty Ponies that I bought in the charity shop and I decided that today was the day that Sam ought to learn the consequences of his behaviour.

Fortunately, Sam was having his disgusting little friends over today. He only ever invites the same sad little boys around. I think he's only got two friends. I suspect that they've all ended up together because no one else at school will talk to them.

Anyway, while Sam was answering the door, I put my plan into action. I heard them come thundering up the stairs and then the spindly one said, 'Sam! What are those?'

And then the lumpy one said, 'Urrrrr, gross! Sam loves Pretty Ponies. He plays with them and plaits their hair!'

Sam was making squeaky noises of rage and came storming into my room and shouted, 'You're so immature!' He threw down the lovely My Pretty Ponies that I had arranged on his windowsill.

Lumpy and Spindly appeared behind Sam to get a good look.

I said, 'Me? Immature? You're the one throwing your toys about.' And then I laughed so hard that I barely noticed him kicking me in the shins.

I finally got rid of him by threatening to show his mates his baby photos and then I rang Megs to discuss my glittering career in the world of comedy. When I got off the phone I strolled past Sam's room where Lumpy was saying, 'Let me show you this brilliant biking website.'

Sam switched on the computer and I crept away. Three seconds later he roared, 'FAITH!' Followed by, 'MUM!'

I don't know what he was getting so worked up about. I think that a real My Pretty Ponies fan like Sam deserves a Pretty Ponies screen saver, don't you?

SUNDAY 30TH OCTOBER

Went to Granny's. I told her Sam would like a My Pretty Pony for his birthday.

LATER

As usual, Mum insisted on food shopping on the way back from Granny's. I keep asking her why she doesn't shop at a proper hippy organic place, but she just says things like, 'They don't have three-for-two offers.' Which seems a bit grasping to me, for a woman who says that happiness is the only real currency in life.

Sam and I wandered off from Mum and Dad so that we could do a spot of milk-boxing. First, you grab yourself a pair of those four-pint plastic milk containers and grip them tightly so that the big fat milk-containing part is covering your knuckles – like a boxing glove – then, you start throwing punches at your opponent. It's extremely funny and very much frowned on by the supermarket staff. That's why the first rule of milk-boxing club is *Don't get caught milk-boxing*. Fortunately, the supermarket is pretty quiet on a Sunday night and most of the staff who were there were teenagers, who were too busy flirting with each other to notice much. (Although I don't know how anyone can manage to flirt while wearing a name badge and one of those bakery-counter hairnets.)

'Here he is!' Sam said. 'It's the Dairy Dynamo, it's the Milky Master, it's . . . Sam Ashby! Taking on his puny opponent—'

'Taking on his nemesis the Belle of the Bottle, it's . . . Face-Smasher Faith.' I added a few whoops at this point, but not too loud because some middle-aged woman was already giving us evil looks.

I swung at Sam and got in a good milk-punch

on his left arm. He tried to get me in the side, but I blocked him and then gave him a smash to the shoulder. A toddler going past in the baby-seat of a trolley gave me a round of applause.

'The crowd's going wild. Face-Smasher is going to win again!'

While I wasn't concentrating, Sam gave me a double blow to the legs. I went for a spinning punch in return, but unfortunately I smacked into Sam's left 'glove' and he sprang a leak. This is the ugly side of milk-boxing. And when milk is spilt you have to follow the second rule of milk-boxing club: *If you make a puddle, slink away.*

So we slunk.

MONDAY 31ST OCTOBER

Most of today has been taken up looking for the perfect mascara – I did have to go to school for a bit, but I tried not to let that distract me from the main aim of the day. At lunchtime Megs and I found a mazzy with a revolutionary formula including elasto-technology and anti-clump recipe. I made an effort to understand the information on the back of the packet. (I have suggested a number of times that we ought to be taught a *Science of Makeup* module at school, but will they listen?)

Megs was not interested in stretching her mind by learning about triple-action thickenisers and kept on about how Miss Ramsbottom had made her stand at the front of the classroom and read out all the mistakes she had made in her homework. 'She's embarrassed Lily and ruined your life. Look at you, all sad and lonely with no rehearsal to go to. Nothing to do on a Friday afternoon. Hanging about like a loser waiting for us to come out . . .'

'Thanks for cheering me up, Megs.'

'. . . And I have to suffer her in the classroom. You're lucky, Faith.'

'Mmm, it's interesting, isn't it? In all the time we've been at this school, I have never had Miss Ramsbottom teaching me. It's almost as if she doesn't want me in her classroom.'

'It's a miserable place to be. She's got some outrageous ideas about us sitting still and completing work and listening to what she is saying and the like.'

'It's amazing they ever let her have a teaching qualification.'

'Can't we do something about her?'

At this point I got a bit cross. 'Do something? All term you've been telling me that I'm *not allowed* to do anything; that I've got to be good so that we can get back in the same tutor group. *And* you and Lily and Angharad tell me that I'm always twisting your arms into doing something, but now you're saying that we *should* do something, are you?'

Megs rubbed her face to wipe off the spit that

I may have accidentally splattered her with in my attempt to get my point across.

'All right, all right. We probably should just leave it.'

But she carried on muttering all the way back to school. I suspect that Megan is tiring of my good behaviour. Thank goodness.

NOVEMBER

NOVEMBER

TUESDAY 1ST NOVEMBER

Miss Ramsbottom has finally gone too far. During assembly she told us that any girl caught wearing mascara to school would be taken to the nearest sink and scrubbed clean. When she announced it we were too horrified to even gasp and then for the rest of the day there was a shocked silence about the place. Zoe kept whispering, 'She can't do it, she just can't,' and Becky burst into tears on more than one occasion.

When we were holed up in the gym cupboard at lunchtime trying to imagine what we'd all look like with albino eyelashes, Megs suddenly burst out, 'That's it, Faith! I am officially giving you permission to scheme against Miss Ramsbottom. Something must be done. She's not content with already being more glamorous than the rest of us; she wants to make us all ugly! Not to mention the fact that she has ripped the joy from your life by banning you from the choir. You are a picture of sadness. You'll probably never marry . . .'

'OK, OK! Let's get her.'

Later on, Megs started worrying about us mucking up our chances of getting back in the same tutor group, but as I said to her, we will not ruin my excellent record of goodness this term because we will not get caught.

WEDNESDAY 2ND NOVEMBER

I've given a lot of thought to Ramsbottom's downfall – mostly while we were in double Physics, which means I have also fulfilled my promise to Dad to use my brain in Science. I've realised that the one person who has the power to make Ramsbottom's life a misery is Miss Pee. All I've got to do is to get Ramsbottom into Miss Pee's bad books and then we can sit back and enjoy her misery.

It's been hard to think of something that would really annoy Miss Pee. She doesn't seem to mind that Miss Ramsbottom is an evil sadist or that she persecutes the ginger who walk amongst us. I've seen Miss Pee watch a Year Eleven tearing a new girl's ear off and all she said was, 'Those earrings aren't regulation, are they, Louise?'

Then it came to me. The one thing Miss Pee holds dear. Her parking space. All I have to do is get Ramsbottom's car into Miss Pee's space and she's dead.

During breaktime (well, Geography, but it's pretty much same thing) Lily asked if I'd come up with a plan to punish Ramsbottom yet.

'Yes, and I will be needing your help. I have surpassed myself,' I said. 'You should start collecting signatures on a farewell card for Ramsbottom right now.'

'I'm not doing anything involving fireworks. I haven't forgotten the last time.'

Which surprised me because sometimes Lily forgets her house number.

'Who said anything about fireworks? This is much better.'

'Eyebrows take a long time to grow back you know.'

'Do not fear! Your caterpillars are safe.'

'And no dogs. Or weedkiller. And if we have to wear disguises Megs can be the vicar this time.'

Too right. Lily's idea of acting is to talk in an accent that switches from Australian to Irish when she gets excited. It didn't seem like she was entering into the right spirit of the thing, which is the spirit of not questioning me.

So I told her, 'You can stay at home and knit if you prefer, or you can witness the spectacular spectacle that will be Miss Pee's face when she finds Ramsbottom's car in her precious parking space.'

'How are we going to do that? We'd have to do driving.'

'Not really driving, more parking.'

'Isn't that supposed to be the hardest part? My mum says reversing into a space is a nightmare.'

I do not wish to cast nasturtiums on Lily's family line, but her mother describes choosing her nail varnish colour as a 'nightmare'.

'It will be fine,' I said. 'Besides I am calling in a specialist to do the driving part.'

In the end Lily agreed to be part of it, although I doubt it will be a working part. The last thing she said was that she hoped my driving specialist wasn't that rubbish lorry driver that I had to make friends with the time that I 'accidentally' threw away my dad's fishing rod.

LATER
Which means I'll have to think of someone else to drive.

EVEN LATER
Because under no circumstances should Lily be proved right. It goes straight to her head and she forgets that she is not to make decisions and that's how we ended up at a Venture Scouts party that time.

WAY LATER
I wouldn't have minded if any of them had been capable of appreciating a good woggle joke.

THURSDAY 3RD NOVEMBER
My scheme is coming along nicely. We had PE this afternoon. Lily and Angharad are in a special group for the terminally noodle-armed and their pixie

friends, so I took the opportunity to have a chat with Zoe. Killer Bill kept rudely interrupting by shouting things like, 'Run, Faith!' and, 'It wouldn't have hit you in the face if you'd been watching the ball'. But we managed mostly to ignore her.

Zoe has had an idyllic childhood. She lives on her father's vast and valuable farm. I can only think that I may have grown up a better person if I had lived somewhere vast and valuable. It's also possible that I might have enjoyed having a pony, learning to drive a tractor and frolicking in the fields with handsome stable lads and the like. Yes, I sometimes think the country life could have been the making of me.

And then I think about living fifty miles from a Topshop and I come to my senses. But Zoe is a useful girl to know.

I told her this and she said, 'You can't have another baby chick. Not after what happened to the last one . . .'

'I don't want a chick.'

'I mean, it must have been quite traumatic being sellotaped inside an eggshell just so you could scare the Food Tech teacher.'

'I do not want a chick – unless you have a few going spare? What I need are your sweet skills,' I said.

'Sorry, Faith, I promised my dad no more forgery this term.'

'I don't want you to forge anything! What do you think I am? Some sort of criminal overlord? I just want you to break into and drive a car.'

'Faith, is this one of your mad schemes that seems like a justifiable act of revenge against the evil rulers of this school, but ends in utter chaos, destruction and occasionally hospitalisation?'

'It might be.'

'Brilliant. I'll drive,' she said.

LATER

I did enquire if living on a farm had also equipped Zoe with hot-wiring skills, but it seems that this is not the case. Which means that I will have to get hold of Ramsbottom's car keys. I also need to see Miss Pee's diary so I can find a day when she needs to leave school, but comes back before Miss Ramsbottom wants to leave and finds her car has been moved. This means gaining access to Miss Pee's office.

Not a problem.

In fact usually I find the difficulty is keeping out of it.

FRIDAY 4TH NOVEMBER

I am not well. I am not at all well. Have I mentioned that I am not feeling well? I have been extremely ill.

Megs phoned me at lunchtime to find out why I wasn't at school and I explained my affliction as delicately as I could. I said, 'Today I have felt grateful for our tiny bathroom and the fact that the loo is so close to the sink.'

'Eeuh! Faith, do you mean it was coming out of both ends?'

Megs is not delicate. When I go to Finishing School to learn how to drink champagne and meet rich men called Henry, they probably won't let her in the door when she comes to visit.

I used my gentle persuasion to tell Megs to change the subject. I said, 'Shut your filthy trap and tell me what I am missing.'

'We tied the stuffed crocodile from Mrs Mac's room to Ang's back and got her to slither around on the floor.'

'Sounds terrifying.'

'The Year Sevens thought so when she chased them down the corridor.'

'I forbid you to do anything else fun before I come back.'

'Hmm. That's not a promise I can make. This afternoon we've got Art with that drippy supply teacher. I'm just off to pick up the party snacks now.'

Why does everything good happen when I'm trapped in a small room? All I need to complete this scene is for Ramsbottom's head to pop up out of the loo.

She can do that you know.

LATER

They'll have finished rehearsal and be heading off to Juicy Lucy's now. Laughing and joking. Not thinking about me. I hate that lot.

LATER STILL

I have always loved my mates. I've just received seven text messages. Megs, Ang, Lily, Zoe and Becky all sent their best love and hoped I'd feel better soon. Westy sent me a picture of himself giving Elliot a wedgie. The last one was from Ethan. Megs must have given him and Westy my number. It said, **Stop skiving you slacker. We need you here to tell Vicky to shut up**.

Strangely, that was my favourite.

SATURDAY 5TH NOVEMBER

I'm feeling a bit better. To celebrate my return to health, people seem to have been setting off fireworks ever since it got dark. How thoughtful.

Mum, Dad and Sam are about to go out to watch a fireworks display in the park. I am still too weak to go with them, besides I am looking forward to being in charge of the remote. I told

Dad to think of me while he's enjoying himself and to bring me back a toffee apple or three. He said he wasn't sure that a toffee apple was a good idea for someone recovering from a stomach bug. I told him I would accept a cash alternative.

Perhaps he's right. I should probably ease myself back into eating solid food by starting with something simple. Like crisps or chocolate.

SUNDAY 6TH NOVEMBER

Granny came round today. She didn't bring me a present, so I'm not sure why she bothered. I said that I should be excused since I'm only just off my deathbed, but Mum just said I could have a blanket on the sofa. I asked if a little light snoozing would be allowed, but she just started tickling me. I told her that tickling a person who has recently been projectile vomiting wasn't advisable, but she didn't stop so I was forced to sit on her. In the middle of this family bonding Granny arrived and started blithering on.

She started by telling us about used-to-be-a-politician Pete, who is her latest gentleman friend who she met at her Elderly Support group. This group seems to consist of Granny and her mates (i.e. *old* people) pretending that they are not old, by organising coffee mornings and mystery tours for people who are even older than they are. It's disgusting really. That would be like me being friends with Icky just so her repulsive ugliness would make me look pretty.

Anyway, Granny started on about this Christmas box business again, 'We've organised a scheme where volunteers are filling nicely-wrapped shoe boxes with treats—'

I said, 'What kind of treats?'

'Oh, toiletries and sweeties and that sort of thing.'

I'm not sure that some Forest Fern talc and a bag of humbugs would make my Christmas.

Granny warbled on, 'And those lovely girls at St Mildred's—'

'Granny, don't be fooled, those girls are savages in tartan kilts.'

Mum said, 'Faith! Don't call them that.'

Granny hadn't heard me. When she's talking I don't think she's actually interested in getting a reply, she just likes to have eyes on her. If we propped up a few of Sam's stuffed animals we could probably leave the room.

On she dribbled. 'Those nice girls are joining in and I hear that they're planning to pack up fifty boxes of treats for the old folks. You know, for some of them it will be the only Christmas gift they get.'

I said, 'I could help.'

Mum, Granny and Sam stared at me open-mouthed. Which I thought was a bit rude as I am well-known for my generosity.

I said, 'I know you're waiting for me to say something mean, but I think it's really sad that old people get forgotten about. Everybody should have presents at Christmas.'

I think Mum might have started welling up at this point.

'I can get the girls at school to help. We'll do loads of boxes, Granny.'

Mum said, 'What a lovely idea, Faith. I've always thought that your aura suggested a caring nature.' Then she took Granny out to the kitchen for a cup of tea to steady their nerves after the shock.

Sam elbowed me in the ribs. He said, 'Why are you being so nice? It makes me feel funny.'

'One day, Sam, you will be moved by the plight of someone else and you'll feel a desire to help them. You'll want to give your time and energy to do something positive. It's really a very good feeling.' I twisted his arm up behind his back and gave him a Chinese burn. 'Besides, if the bimbos in blazers can pack fifty boxes for the coffin-dodgers I reckon we can do a hundred.'

I am such a people person.

MONDAY 7TH NOVEMBER
Despite still feeling rough I was forced to go to school today.

I decided that we need to press ahead with our plans to ruin Miss Ramsbottom. I thought that perhaps I should pop into Miss Pee's office to take a look at her diary, but before I'd even had the chance to decide when would be most convenient for me to drop in on Miss Pee, I was sent to her by Killer Bill for attempting to slide the length of the corridor on two banana skins.

I protested firmly, but politely, 'This is practically sport!' But Killer Bill wasn't listening. Sometimes I think a life of sport with all that being hit on the head by a variety of balls has rendered her deaf to my sensible explanations. I said, 'And I am promoting healthy eating.' Still she sent me off to the Queen Pee. Because I am a positive person I tried to look upon it as good fortune being invited into Miss Pee's lair where I could get a good look at her schedule.

Miss Pee said, 'Faith.' (Nobody else manages to make my name sound quite so much like a growl.) 'What is it this time?'

I handed her the pink misdemeanour slip Killer Bill had written out for me. She smoothed out the long strip and read it. Then she paused.

Miss Pee is fond of pauses. I think she imagines that she is building the tension and that I am writhing in anticipation of the dreadful punishment she will hand out. Actually, I was thinking about sandwiches. I was hoping that Dad hadn't put the tomato next to the bread; you need to sandwich it between the cheese, otherwise it makes the bread all soggy.

Miss Pee said, 'I have had so many of these . . .' she dangled the pink strip between her fingers, '. . . concerning you, Faith, that I could make myself a hula skirt.'

I'm afraid a snort escaped me. You'd giggle if you were confronted with the image of Miss Pee hula-ing around the desk with a giant cocktail, wearing nothing but a rustling skirt of my pink slips. It wouldn't even be that immodest; she could tuck her sagging bosoms in the waistband. *Ewww,* now I have thought about Miss Pee's boobies. I swear she knows what she is saying; even now she's conducting some sort of long-distance mental torture. And it is working.

Anyway, midway through her lecture Miss Pee spotted some Year Sevens out the window where no Year Sevens should be. (In fact no one is allowed anywhere near Miss Pee's window. Which seems odd to me. I do not think that you should become head of an institution full of girls, if just a glimpse of them makes you leap from your chair and shout, 'Off! Off!') She flung open her window and started a new lecture to the Year Sevens on the evilness of being in her sight line.

I spun round the leather diary open on Miss Pee's desk. Quietly, so as to not disturb Miss Pee's enjoyment of the sound of her own voice, I flicked over a few pages. Goodness, let me tell you how exciting Miss Pee's days are: *meeting with governors, meeting with parents, Presentation Evening, site proposal due in*. Boring, boring, boring. Then I found what I was looking for. Friday the eighteenth of November, Miss Pee will be attending a Schools' Alliance meeting at St Mildred's in the morning and has to be back for support staff appraisals by half two. So that means she'll be in school at the start of the day for assembly, then we'll have a great car-moving window while she's at St Mildred's and she'll be back to discover her space taken before it's time for Ramsbottom to leave. Perfect.

TUESDAY 8TH NOVEMBER

I got Mrs Webber to let me make a special announcement in tutor time so I could tell everyone about the Christmas boxes. No one seemed very enthusiastic.

Nicola Robson said, 'I have to buy chocolates for my nan for Christmas, I'm not giving to old people that didn't even give birth to my mum or anything.'

She expects a lot in return for a pack of Ferrero Rocher.

I've only got four groups signed up to do a box.

I won't be able to manage as many tomorrow as my karate arm is sore from persuading the first lot.

WEDNESDAY 9TH NOVEMBER

I had a rummage through our house this evening in search of shoeboxes that I can fill with treats for the old people. I found one in Mum's wardrobe with the most hideous pair of Marks and Spencer's sandals in. I was tempted to leave the sandals in there and to wrap it straight away. They seemed like the kind of footwear an old person would enjoy. But instead I crammed the shoes behind the folded-up exercise bike (she'll never look there).

I found another shoebox under Sam's bed, but the smell coming off it was so bad that I put it straight back. And then there was one in my room that was housing my cracker joke collection, but I've moved those into my knicker drawer. Which means I've got two shoeboxes. Great. I wonder if the old folks would like their gifts in a cereal box. Or a nice festive carrier bag?

THURSDAY 10TH NOVEMBER

Mrs Webber brought in four empty shoeboxes.

I said, 'Thank you very much, Mrs W. It's

touching that an elderly person such as yourself finds the time to support other old codgers.'

She said, 'Faith, I'm thirty-seven.'

'Try not to dwell on it, Mrs W; old age comes to us all.'

And then I handed out the newsletters for her without being asked, to show her how pleased I was.

Hope she brings something to put in them tomorrow.

FRIDAY 11TH NOVEMBER

Ahhhhhh! and *Eeeeeeee!* And a bit of can-can dancing. Finn has asked me out!

Yes, actual Finn has actually asked me out. I'm so excited I can hardly write. I met up with the others after rehearsal and we went to Juicy Lucy's. Finn just happened to be sitting on the table next to us and I just happened to get into a conversation with him about surfing (because, as you know, I have always been a big fan) and he said, 'There's this really cool website. Give me your number and I'll text it to you.'

He wanted my number! *Woo hoo!*

Which isn't what I said, what I said was, 'Sure,' because I wanted to be cool.

Finn asking me for my number and telling me about his favourite website seemed quite exciting, until just now when I got a text from a number that I didn't recognise. I opened it thinking it might be one of those scam ones you get pretending to be your bank saying, **Just text us your PIN and your date of birth and tell us where you hide the spare front door key**, but it wasn't. It was from Finn. As soon as I opened it I saw his name at the end. I had to steady myself before I could even read the rest of it, but there it was: *he was asking me to go to the cinema tomorrow night*. Phew, must remember to keep breathing. I waited for a suitable period of time (six and a half minutes) before replying and there we go – I've got a date. With Finn. Oh my giant bra-ed grandmother, I cannot believe it.

SATURDAY 12TH NOVEMBER

The problem with going on a date is that there is no one to ring and ask what they are wearing. I rang Megs last night; I could tell she was pleased for me because she screamed. I was quite touched, so I screamed back.

Dad said, 'Do you really need to be on the phone to do that? She's only a few streets away. If you put down the phone she'd probably still be able to hear you.'

When he'd finished his meaningless babble, I asked Megs what I should wear. She said she thought casual was best.

I said, 'Casual by whose standard? Icky thinks a backless cocktail dress is casual. She thinks getting dressed up is remembering to put your underwear on.'

'Properly casual. Like jeans casual.'

Which I took to mean a denim mini.

LATER

It's only six hours to go. All I have to do is keep breathing till then. It would be just my luck to drop dead just before my very first date. And maybe my first snog. *Eeep!* Is he going to kiss me? Think I've just increased my chances of a heart attack.

MORE LATE

I'm ready.

I'd be more ready if I felt better qualified for this. They should offer a GCSE in kissing and a BTEC in flirting.

I've cleaned my teeth twice and practised looking attractive in the dark sideways on. Time to go.

SUNDAY 13TH NOVEMBER

That's it. I am never going to school again.

It was a trick.

Evil Ethan is probably still laughing his stupid curly head off now.

I got to the cinema a little bit early. I didn't want to look over-enthusiastic, so I sort of skulked about pretending to be interested in the nearest shop. Then I realised it was a chemist's and I was eyeing up the display of incontinence pants, so I walked very slowly towards the cinema entrance and started reading the posters. I was studying the reviews for *The Sunshine Bears' Birthday Surprise* for the third time when suddenly Finn appeared leaning against a pillar, as laid-back and relaxed as ever.

He said, 'Oh, hey, Faith.'

Looking back, I realise now that he seemed a bit surprised to see me. I should have paid more attention to this and I should not have said, 'So what are we going to see?'

'We? Uh . . . I'm actually going with these guys, but you could—'

I spun round in the direction he was pointing and there were two of his mates and three girls. One of whom was Icky bleeping Blundell. At this point I tried to use the heat coming off my red face to power my teleportation, but nothing happened.

Icky skipped up to us with a delighted expression. 'Oh, poor Faith, have you been stood up? Well, don't start crying on Finn's shoulder. Even your poodle-haired loser friend doesn't want you. Finn's way out of your league.'

Finn started asking who was a poodle or something, but I was already stalking off. Icky was wrong. That poodle-haired Ethan hadn't stood me up. He'd *set* me up. He must have sent me that text and he must have known that this lot were meeting at the cinema. How could he be such a pig? I stormed around the corner and slammed straight into what I thought was a wall, but turned out to be Westy.

'Faith!' Then he saw my face. 'Hey, what's the matter?'

Annoyingly, I'd started to well up with tears. Poor old Westy didn't know what to do. He went bright red and gave me a pat on the shoulder, except he doesn't know his own strength so I nearly fell over.

I pulled myself together a bit and said, 'You can tell Ethan that I didn't think that his joke was very funny.'

'Ethan?'

'Yes, Ethan. He sent me a text pretending to be Finn, asking me out. I bet he thinks he's hilarious.'

'Oh, this is bad. Listen, Faith—'

I could see a gaggle of girls from school heading towards the cinema and I didn't want anyone else to witness my humiliation and blotchy face so I said to Westy, 'Never mind. See you later.'

He said, 'Wait a minute, Faith, I hate seeing

you upset. Can I ... Can I buy you a drink or something?'

Oh my, I have sunk so low that Westy was trying to make me feel better. I didn't want to hear it. I came home and climbed into bed, where I will be living out the rest of my natural life.

MONDAY 14TH NOVEMBER
Awful day. I don't want to talk about it.

LATER
Queen of the evil gnomes, Icky Blundell, has told the world that I was stood up. The only good thing about it is that she seems to think that it was Ethan who stood me up. Finn obviously didn't tell her that I was expecting to see the film with him, which makes him a very nice person, but I'll never be able to be in the same room as him again, so his niceness is wasted. Also, here's a question: was Finn going to the cinema with Icky? I mean I know they were both there, but were they *together* together? Because that detracts from his niceness. No one nice could want to spend time with Icky.

All day long I have suffered Icky's annoying mates telling me they're not surprised I was stood up because I am so ugly/ginger/flat-chested. Then the word spread and one of the Year Eleven Tarty Party actually took time out of her busy schedule of spot-squeezing and horoscope-reading to come and say to me, 'Who'd want to go out with you? You're so minging and . . . brainy.'

Seriously. The fact that the Tarty Party consider brains a turn-off explains a lot about the slack-jawed ape-boys that they like to date.

I said to her, 'Most people find intelligence attractive.'

'They don't put pictures of girls with big brains on the front of magazines, do they?' she said and walked off smirking.

And then to top it all off, Angharad – little, tiny, never had a sniff of a date – Angharad *looked at me sympathetically.*

So I said, 'If you look at me like that again I will strangle you with your own shoelaces.'

Which is no way to talk to a friend who is more mouse than girl and who was only trying to be nice. It's a good job she didn't try to put her arm around me. She'd have been hospitalised.

LATER STILL

This is Ethan's fault. What kind of a worm brings people's emotions into a joke? In fact, where is the joke? I don't remember Finn laughing. I'm definitely not laughing. Becky did give a nervous giggle when I told her, but that soon stopped when I stood on her windpipe. The only person laughing is Icky. And we all know she laughs at drowning puppies. I kicked her in the shins on two occasions today, but that only stopped her going on about me being stood up for about five seconds.

Nasty, pig-face Ethan. I will never forgive him. I will not forget this till my dying day. I am exhausted by the humiliation, the cruelty and all the punching people in the face that I have had to do today.

But, like I said, I don't want to talk about it.

TUESDAY 15TH NOVEMBER

The girls took me into town at lunchtime to buy me a milkshake to cheer me. Outside the milkshake place I spotted the unmistakable bear-shape of Westy.

I said, 'Hi, Westy.'

He jumped and said, 'Oh, Faith! Are you . . . Are you all right?'

He looked so worried when he saw me that I said, 'It's OK, Westy, I've got over the blubbing stage. Now I'm just murderously angry.'

'You shouldn't be cross with Ethan,' he said. 'It wa—'

'Yes she should,' Ethan said, appearing from behind me. 'Listen, Faith, I tried to catch you after school yesterday, but you'd already gone. I wanted to explain. It was a really stupid thing for me to do. I just got carried away. I'm sorry.'

I didn't know what to say. I was so angry, but

I couldn't lose it in the middle of the street. I just wanted to get away from him. I could only manage to say, 'It wasn't funny.' And then I rushed inside the milkshake place to find Megs. She'd been watching through the window.

'Did Ethan say sorry?' she asked. 'He looked sorry.'

'I don't care. Has he gone? Have they gone?'

She peered out the window. 'No, looks like Westy is telling Ethan off.'

'Good,' I said. 'He deserves it.'

Ethan and Westy left after a bit and I went back to school feeling worse than ever.

WEDNESDAY 16TH NOVEMBER

Today my spirits had revived enough to have an arm wrestle with Lily during registration. Mrs Webber had just bet Angharad a Rich Tea biscuit that I would win (I've always said that Mrs Webber has a good eye for talent) when Miss Ramsbottom stropped into the room and took me outside for a 'little chat'.

'Faith,' she said, 'I'm hearing stories about violent scuffles between you and another girl over the last couple of days.'

I wanted to stop her right there and point out that Icky is more toad than girl, but I bit my tongue.

'And walking into the classroom just now I

can see that you are still behaving in an overly aggressive fashion. It needs to stop.'

Well. She'd already been extremely annoying, but Ramsbottom always has to take it to another level, so then she said, 'I do hope you're not allowing disappointments in your private life to affect your conduct in school.'

Disappointments in my private life? Does she mean this business with Finn? Who exactly is talking to Miss Ramsbottom about my private life? It's not very private if my head of year is bringing it into the conversation, is it? While I was trying to stop my head exploding from rage, she said, 'I shouldn't need to remind you that I am closely monitoring your behaviour. Make sure you give me no further cause for concern.'

And then she was off. Unbelievable. How dare she? How dare she think that she can go around talking about me getting stood up? Which isn't even what happened! My humiliation couldn't get any deeper.

I can't wait to see Miss Ramsbottom get her own dose of humiliation when we put the car plan into action.

THURSDAY 17TH NOVEMBER

Tomorrow is the day of the big car-moving scam. Megs is having second thoughts again and back-pedalling as fast as skinny-but-thick Sammie used to on the exercise bike before she realised it could go forwards too. Tough. After that embarrassing conversation yesterday I can't wait to pay Ramsbottom back. Besides, I am quietly hoping that if I can get myself known as the girl who got one over on Ramsbottom people will forget I am a sad loser.

FRIDAY 18TH NOVEMBER

Oh, hell on a lollipop stick. The great car-moving extravaganza did not go according to plan.

For starters, our driver, Zoe, was not at school today. We found out later that she's got food poisoning, which is really childish of her. I need to get some new friends who are more professional in their outlook.

Megs wanted to abandon the whole thing or at least wait for Zoe, but there was no way I was going to postpone after all this build-up, so I said I could do the driving part. Megs could see I was not to be trifled with (actually what she said was, 'You're going to keep whining until I do it, aren't you?') so she agreed to go ahead. She even managed to get Ramsbottom's car keys out of her handbag during Geography by causing a diversion (she got Becky to pretend to vomit by spitting up a mouthful of vegetable soup).

At the start of lunch when everyone was busy eating, we snuck around to the front of building. Lily stayed on lookout. (Ang started to hyperventilate when I said I wanted to play a trick on Miss Ramsbottom, so I thought it best to leave her out of it.) Miss Pee's car was gone, just as we expected it to be, and there was Miss Ramsbottom's shiny red car a bit further away in the spaces for less important people. Megs and I got in. Then we heard a *beepy-beep beep-beep* and Megs jumped so much that she hit her head. It was my phone.

I said, 'I'll just see who that is.'

'Do you have to? We are kind of in the middle of something.'

'Megs, I'm not saying that it's the most convenient time, but you know what Hollywood producers are like. When they need a star they call up day or night.'

'What exactly is a Hollywood producer going to want you for?'

'I'm open to both film and TV roles.'

'And where is this producer supposed to have seen you?'

'You know, out and about.' I wiggled my phone out of my pocket.

Megs said, 'And how is your mum?'

It wasn't my mum. It was Lily. It said: **Good luck** ☺

I looked up and there she was, ten metres away, giving me a thumbs up. Honestly. The great train robbers didn't have to put up with this.

I put the keys in the ignition and tried to start up the car. Nothing happened.

Megs said, 'Are you sure about this?'

I said, 'It's fine! My dad once talked me through the basics of driving and I was very nearly listening, so I know what I'm doing.'

On the third attempt the stupid thing finally started. Megs said, 'Now what?'

'I have to get the waggly thing into position.'

'The "waggly thing"? Well it's nice to know that I'm travelling with an expert.'

'Where's the "R"?'

'What?'

'I've got to get the waggly thing into the "R" position, so we can go backwards. You know, "R" for—'

'Rewind?'

'Reverse, you idiot. Jeez, I'm starting to look like a Formula One driver around you.'

'Go on then, do your reversing.'

So I did. I reversed brilliantly. The only problem was that I couldn't stop. Then Megs started squealing and no one could be expected to concentrate with that racket going on and then … SCRUNCH. We'd ploughed straight into the bushes behind us. Being the sensible type I am, I managed to remain calm and let out only a moderate stream of swearing. I hoped Megs would be sensible too, but she started gabbling, 'What the hell have you done? We're in so much trouble. Why did I ever let you talk me into this . . .' etc., etc.

I said, 'Don't panic. All I need to do is—'

Megs shouted, 'Stop! Don't do anything else. I am getting out and so are you.'

So, because I wanted to check out the damage, not because I was doing what Megs told me to, I got out. The back end of the car was entirely in the bushes. I said, 'Bushes are soft. It's probably fine.'

'So you think all those crunching noises were just baby rabbits being run over?'

'Don't be sarcastic, Megs, it makes you look petty.'

'Don't drive, Faith. It makes you look like a killing machine.'

Clearly Megs was hysterical and I would have been perfectly within my rights to give her a slap. Instead I tried to get her to focus on the matter in hand, so I said politely but firmly, 'Shut the hell up and think, Megs.'

We stared at the car. I said, 'All I need to do really is drive it forward.'

'I'm not sure you can manage the drive bit, let

alone deciding which direction it's going in,' Megs said.

'Let's just try.'

'You're not getting back in that car.'

Then Lily whistled the secret whistle. (It wasn't very secret, it was just a whistle, but Lily isn't blessed when it comes to imagination.) Someone was coming. I turned round and found myself nose to nose with Ethan. Where did he spring from? And why is Lily's idea of warning you someone is coming to whistle when they're about to tread on your heels? I said, 'What are you doing here?'

He said, 'Oh, I've been hanging about all day on the off-chance that you might have time to yell in my face. Thanks for the opportunity. Pleasure working with you.'

'What is your problem? Do you enjoy seeing me in embarrassing situations?'

'Faith, I wanted to talk to you. But maybe I should give you a hand with this first.'

He gestured to the car.

I glared at him. Why would I want his help? Does he think that I'm just going to forget about the whole cinema thing?

'I don't want anything from a pig like you.'

'Give me the keys,' he said.

Megs snatched them out of my hand and gave

them to him. He just jumped in the car, started it, and nipped it back into Miss Ramsbottom's space. I have to admit I was quite relieved.

Megs said, 'Oh thank you, Ethan, thank you so much.'

He was looking at me like he expected a medal or something, but just because he'd put the car back it doesn't make up for what he did. Besides, I could have sorted that car out. Probably.

Megs went on squeaking, 'I can't believe you just drove it like that. And now you can't even tell we moved it.' She brushed a leaf off the back end of the car.

Ethan said, 'Yeah, except for that scratch. Was that there before?'

He was right. There was a big scratch above the back right wheel. It was quite noticeable in the red paint.

We stared at it.

Ethan said, 'Have you got any lipstick?'

I said, 'What kind of a stupid question is that? Do think that just because we're girls that—'

'Coral Blush, Strawberry Fizz or Scarlet Lady?' Megs asked.

Stupid Megs.

Ethan took the Scarlet Lady and ran it over the scratch. It disappeared. You could only see it when you were trying. It was pretty clever, even if he is a smug git.

He said, 'It won't last, but it means it might not be noticed today. If they don't see the scratch until later they might not realise it happened at school.' He turned his big eyes full on me. 'Faith, do you think we could have a chat?'

'No. Absolutely not. I never want to speak to you again.'

So then he went.

Megs said, 'You could have heard what he had to say. That was really nice of him. He saved our behinds.'

I meant to say something tough, but what I came up with was, 'I can handle my own behind.'

LATER

We got Ramsbottom's keys back in her bag safely. Lily stood outside her classroom and shouted, 'Squirrel!' really loudly. When Ramsbottom came out to see what was going on, Megs nipped in and returned the keys. Ramsbottom said, 'Lily, what on earth is all this screeching about? A squirrel is hardly cause for such hysteria.'

I said, 'Miss Ramsbottom, Lily lives in a flat on the Caldershot estate. I don't think we should deprive her of the joy of experiencing nature for the first time, do you?'

Then we legged it because I feared Ramsbottom would suggest we get close to nature by picking litter out of it on the field.

Megs couldn't stop gushing about Ethan. She says he's nice. She even asked if I was sure that it was him that sent me that text message pretending to be Finn. She says I am being ungrateful. I *am* grateful. It's just that I'm annoyed as well. That sort of helpful behaviour is unforgivable in someone you are trying to despise.

I don't want to think about Ethan at the moment. I've got other things on my mind. I am actually a teeny bit scared that this whole car thing will be discovered. I wanted to text Lily to ask her again if she's sure that no one saw us, but I've left my phone at school. All afternoon I kept imagining Miss Pee appearing in the doorway of the classroom and taking me away to permanently exclude me and to say some quite unkind things about my levels of stupidity. But she didn't come.

The only unusual thing that happened this afternoon was that Limp Lizzie started to nod off in RE while she had a pencil up her nose. She jerked forward and gave herself a nasty poke. She was lucky enough to draw blood and I was lucky enough to notice first. (Whenever anyone bleeds, or faints, or comes over a bit poorly in a lesson there is always a scrum to get to be the person who takes them to the sick room.) I got to haul Lizzie down the corridor, which meant I missed a chunk of RE. Which is not really that out of the ordinary. I usually manage to miss at least a bit. Even if it's just by putting my fingers in my ears and humming 'I'm a little Teapot'.

SATURDAY 19TH NOVEMBER

Megs came round this morning. She said that Ethan is still waiting to talk to me. She also said that maybe it was all a 'misunderstanding'. Yeah right.

I don't care how sorry Ethan is. It's not good enough. I don't know what hurts most. The fact that he is not as nice and as sensitive as I thought he was, or the fact that he obviously doesn't like me as much as I thought he did. I've been an idiot.

SUNDAY 20TH NOVEMBER

Mum insisted on going to Granny's this afternoon. The rest of my family had settled themselves in the sitting room while I was still moping in the hall, unable to muster the energy to take my coat off. Granny took a good look at me and said, 'Why the long face? Is it man trouble?'

I said nothing, but Granny can smell these things.

'Oh dear,' she said and patted me on the

arm. For a moment I thought she was going to be sympathetic but then the pat turned into a little shake and she said, 'No more crying! Forget him right now!'

I opened my mouth to tell her that the only thing I really needed to forget was my own humiliation, but Granny cut me off.

'Not a word! Don't speak his name. You're much better than him. Now turn around and head towards a brighter future.' She marched me into the other room.

For a little while I actually felt better. As if maybe there might be some hope after this disaster. But I soon started to feel miserable again.

After all, I don't think that watching *Songs of Praise* and fighting Granny for the last Jammie Dodger can really be described as a brighter future.

LATER

We had to make the usual thrilling detour to the Tesco near Granny's house. I bumped into Lily by the fish counter. She didn't bother with a 'Hello', she just said, 'You'd think that all the water in the sea would wash away their fishy smell, wouldn't you?'

I thought *that* was ridiculous comment until she made her next remark. She said, 'I think we should confess.'

I said, 'And I think we shouldn't. As we all know, I'm in charge, so let us never speak of this again.'

'I just think it might look better for us if we own up rather than if they find out we're responsible.'

'How will anyone find out? They don't know there's anything to be responsible for!'

'Yes. Well. I'm warning you now that I'm not a very good liar.'

She's not wrong there. Once Ramsbottom asked her why she was holding a water bomb and Lily said, 'It's not a water bomb, it's a rabbit.'

MONDAY 21ST NOVEMBER

I was quite nervous about school this morning. I had visions of being met at the door and handcuffed by Ramsbottom. Everything seemed all right until assembly when Miss Pee mentioned that she thought that the front hedges were looking rather ragged. She said we weren't to spend our time loitering at the front of the school. I wonder how she feels about us driving stolen vehicles at the front of the school. It was quite funny.

Angharad sucked in her breath and whispered, 'Was that your trick? Did you jump in the bushes?'

Megs and I got the giggles and I had to put a glove in my mouth to stop me from exploding with laughter, then Lily kicked me in the shins, which really set Megs off. At this point Miss Ramsbottom just glided up beside us. (You know, she doesn't make any noise when she moves and I've never seen her shadow . . . I'm just saying.) She didn't tell us off, she just stood there. Like a silent threat. We all pulled ourselves together and bit our lips and watched Miss Pee with great interest (she did say something a bit worrying about her investigating which girls have been breaking the rules by hanging around the front), but my insides were spasming with the effort of not laughing.

As soon as assembly finished we walk-ran out of the hall, clutching on to each other. Then I had to lie down on the stairs and cry with laughter. When Megs finally got enough air into her lungs to speak she said, 'Lily! You finished me off when you started on Faith. I thought she was going to choke on that glove. What did you kick her for?'

Lily gave me a smack around the back of the head. 'It was my glove.'

LATER

I've completely lost my mobile. It's not at school. It's really annoying. Anyone could be trying to call me and offer me a part in a musical or to ask me to turn on some Christmas lights. They'll think I'm not interested. This wouldn't have happened if Mum and Dad had got me a secretary for Christmas like I asked.

LATER STILL

Mum has found out about my phone. She was making a delightful vegetarian tea of lentils and old mattress pie or something, and I was pouring all my energy and attention into my Maths homework whilst making a sandwich and watching a bit of TV, when I realised that Megs had my calculator. Obviously, I couldn't use my phone, so I decided to include my dear brother in my quest for learning by encouraging him to use his mind with me.

I said, 'You there, boy! What's the square root of one thousand two hundred and twenty-five?' Somehow Sam's whining and lack of numeracy ended up with me having to explain why I was missing various bits of equipment to Mum. She's not happy about the lost phone.

She said, 'Where did you have it last?'

'If I knew where I had it last, I would go to that place and pick it up and then it wouldn't be lost, and there would be the added advantage that I wouldn't be having this silly conversation with you anymore.'

Mum said that young people need to learn to take care of things and no wonder the planet is in such a state when kids have a throwaway attitude towards possessions.

I said, 'Tell you what, if you give me the cash I'll nip out and get a new one now.'

She hit me over the head with a packet of wholewheat pasta.

MIDDLE OF THE NIGHT

I have remembered where I had my phone last.

It was in Ramsbottom's car.

TUESDAY 22ND NOVEMBER

This morning all I could think about was my phone. At breaktime I poured the whole story out to the gang.

Lily said, 'But how will she even know it's yours ...' Then she trailed off because actually my poor moby has spent quite a lot of time in Miss Ramsbottom's possession. She confiscates it whenever she can. And those purple zebra stripes are quite striking.

I sank into a fog of depression and fear at that point. Unfortunately, we had PE next so no one was very sympathetic because they were all feeling the same sort of thing.

At lunchtime Megs, Lily and I slipped past the prefects on guard to the front of the school. (Actually I said, 'All right, Josie? Do you want one of Lily's Maltesers?') We had a good peer into Ramsbottom's car; there was no sign of my phone. I got Lily to ring me but we couldn't hear a thing.

So I'm still stuck. Ramsbottom might have it. She might not. The stress is making my hair frizzy.

WEDNESDAY 23RD NOVEMBER

Today the moment I had been dreading arrived. At breaktime Limp Lizzie flopped her way towards me and said, 'Miss Ramsbottom told me to find you—'

'And you have. Well done. This time, give me a ten-minute start and we'll put your superior tracking skills to the test again.'

'No, wait, she wants to see you.'

'Miss Ramsbottom also wants to see the undead take over the earth. I'm not sure we should give in to her every whim.'

By this point Lizzie was wild-eyed with terror at the thought that she might not be able to persuade me to toddle off and see Miss Ramsbottom, but to be honest with you the fight had gone out of me. I gave myself up and slunk off to Ramsbottom's vault after giving Lizzie only a very token Chinese burn.

When I got there Ramsbottom put down her mid-morning snack (I think it was the leg of a gazelle) and turned her eyes full beam on me.

'Tell me, Faith, why do you think you are here?'

I wasn't falling for that one. There's nothing dignified about confessing. So I said, 'Is it because you want to recognise my ongoing contribution to high fashion standards under difficult circumstances?'

She flared her nostrils.

And held up my mobile.

It was a bit like those dreams you have when you're falling off a balcony. All I could do was brace myself for impact.

'Faith, do you know where I found this?'

In an attempt to look innocent I did my Bambi impression.

Ramsbottom said, 'Well, it wasn't switched off and at the bottom of your bag. Which, as you well know, is the only place that mobiles are permitted in school.'

I wondered exactly what the punishment for driving your teacher's car would be. I was definitely going to get excluded and before that Ramsbottom would probably tar and feather me.

'There is a rule forbidding girls to loiter at the front of the school.'

I squeezed my eyes shut and waited for her to say: *Also not permitted is driving my car just because you're a bit annoyed with me.*

But she didn't.

Instead she said, 'Your phone was found in the covered walkway leading to the front of school. What have you got to say for yourself?'

Ha ha! I know something you don't know! didn't seem entirely appropriate so I said, 'When the snow is driving and the wind is particularly biting I do sometimes gather Year Sevens in the covered walkway to stop them from freezing to death.'

'It seems interesting to me that your phone was found so close to those damaged bushes. Faith, if you are serious about being allowed to return to your former tutor group then I suggest that you cause no further trouble this term. Am I making myself clear?'

I nodded.

'You'd better get back to class. You can pick up your phone from me at the end of the day.'

'Yes, Miss. I'll be on my best behaviour, Miss.'

Then she quite rudely hustled me out of her lair.

As the door was closing I did ask, 'Were there any messages?' but she pretended not to hear me.

LATER
When I finally got my phone back, I was excited to look through my texts, hoping that there would be a few from attractive boys, or at the very least some offers to do Christmas boxes. All I got was

various dribblings on from Megs and a photo of a monkey from Lily.

THURSDAY 24TH NOVEMBER

I can't believe what's happened today. Can my life get any more ridiculous? I was trying to put my recent nightmare behind me by moaning on about it to Megs when she said, 'Are you going to meet us after rehearsal tomorrow?'

I said, 'No, Ethan will be there.'

Megs pursed her lips. 'Are you actually sure that it was him that sent that message?'

'Yes, he's the one who plays tricks, isn't he? Remember the chilli?'

'But that was different to this. Does he even have your number?'

I thought about this. 'Yes! He does, he sent me that text when I was ill. You must have given him my number.'

'Nope, not me.'

'Well, maybe it was Lily.' Then I remembered something else. 'I've deleted his text pretending to be Finn, but I remember that the number it came from ended in a double six.' I whipped out my phone. 'And I bet you that that text from Ethan when I was sick does too.' I scrolled back through my messages while Megs leant over my shoulder. I got to the right day and there it was: a text from a number ending in double six. I gave Megs a triumphant smirk and opened the message.

But it wasn't the text from Ethan.

It was the one from Westy.

'See!' Megs said. 'I knew it wasn't Ethan.'

'He could have used Westy's phone.' But even as I was saying it I knew that it wasn't true. It makes perfect sense that Westy sent the text. It explains why he was at the cinema and why he's been a bit weirdy ever since. But *why* would he do a mean thing like that?

Megs says he probably didn't mean to upset me, but I am upset. Everything is horrible. I feel bad that I was cross with Ethan, but somehow I'm still angry with him too. Why did he let me think it was him? I'm exhausted. I'm going to bed and I might not get out again till spring.

FRIDAY 25TH NOVEMBER

I told Dad that I was too unwell to go to school today.

He said, 'What's wrong with you?'

I said, 'I have a battered spirit and a bruised belief in humankind.'

'That's lucky; I thought you'd got this flu that's going around.'

'Dad! I'm depressed! Don't you have any words of fatherly advice?'

He had a think about it. 'Your mum's in the kitchen.'

Mum made me a cup of what looked like pond-water tea (didn't help at all) and gave me a cuddle (helped a bit).

I dragged myself to school and started to explore and explain my woes to Megs using all of my language skills, i.e. I said, 'Waaaaaaaaaaaaaaaaaaaaahh.'

Megs sat up straight, which is never a good sign, and said, 'Faith, listen to me. I know all this has been embarrassing, but you need to get over it. No one ever really knew that you thought Finn had asked you out and no one is even talking about you looking lonely at the cinema anymore. Let's move on to the next thing, shall we? We need to think about the Christmas boxes, yes?'

I'm afraid that my lip started to wobble at that point. 'Don't you care that I have been humiliated? Don't you care that I'm sad?'

'Of course I care, you custard cream. That is why I'm not going to let you get this out of proportion. I don't want it to be like the time you didn't get to be the angel Gabriel in the nativity all over again.'

I sniffed. 'That was primary school. You weren't even there for that.'

'No, but the fact that you were still explaining your conspiracy theories about it in Year Seven, suggests that you didn't handle it that well. Listen to me, Faith. No one is laughing at you. Ethan is a nice boy who likes you and who probably only let you think he'd messed with you to protect his friend Westy. And Westy . . . Well, Westy wouldn't want to upset anyone, would he?'

I shook my head.

'So let's forget about it. After rehearsal we'll go to Juicy Lucy's and just have a nice time with our mates. You don't have to talk to Ethan and Westy if you don't want to, OK?'

'OK.'

Then she gave me a squeeze and I said, 'You're quite smart really, Megs.'

She nodded wisely.

'Don't tell anyone, though,' I said. 'They'd never believe you.'

LATER

So I decided I would go to Juicy Lucy's. I can't let some stupid boys spoil my social life. All afternoon I kept thinking about what I wanted to say to Westy and Ethan. At first I thought that I'd try and avoid them, but then I decided that I wanted some answers. Even so, it still gave me a shock when the first person I saw when I walked into Juicy Lucy's was Ethan.

I stared at him in horror.

He said, 'I'm going to assume that you're looking at me like that because you're transfixed by my good looks.'

'Why did you let me think it was you?' I blurted out.

'Why did I what?'

'I know it was Westy who sent that text pretending to be Finn.'

'Oh.'

'You shouldn't have said it was you.'

'I didn't, you just assumed.'

'So? I once assumed that only men had facial hair, which meant the first time I met my Maths teacher I called her "sir". I shouldn't be allowed to run around assuming things. Why didn't you tell me it was Westy?'

'He was terrified about how you'd react. I just . . . didn't deny what you thought.'

I shook my head. It's very unpleasant realising that you've been cross with someone who was actually being noble.

'Well, I'm sorry if I wasn't very nice to you when I thought it was you.' I didn't sound very sorry, I still sounded cross. That's probably because I was.

He was quite gracious and said, 'That's all right. So . . . how are you?'

'Fine,' I said stiffly and completely untruthfully. 'You?'

'Yeah, fine.' He grinned at me. 'Since we're baring our souls. You know it's not the same without you at choir.'

'I expect Icky's making enough noise for me.'

He said, 'Sometimes I think that there's some sort of alien living inside her with its hand wrapped round her windpipe. It's not natural for a person to make a noise that high-pitched.'

'Alien … tapeworm … there's definitely something inside her consuming all her food.'

'Drinking her milk of human kindness.'

'Strangling her sense of decency.'

Just then we heard Icky's voice outside the café screeching, 'DAAAAAAAAN!'

We cracked up. Which helped a bit with all the weirdness.

Lily leant over and said, 'Icky's in a bad mood because Finn isn't paying her any attention. He came over to her today and she was all excited and putting on her super-pout and he just asked her where you were. She was so annoyed.'

'Really? Finn was asking about me? What did he say?'

Apparently Finn asked both Icky and Lily where I was. He told Lily to say 'Hi'. This is amazing. Even though I must have looked a right idiot at the cinema, he is thinking about me when I'm not there and he's sending me messages. He'll be proposing next.

By the time I'd managed to squeeze all this out of Lily (she got distracted by the idea of vegetarian sausages at one point) Ethan had disappeared. That's when Westy shuffled up to me.

'Faith,' he said. 'Oh Faith, I'm so sorry. I'm an idiot. I know I'm an idiot.'

He looked mortified, he really did, but I was still cross.

'There's a difference between having a bit of a joke and messing with someone's feelings.'

'I know. I'm sorry I just didn't think it through. I didn't realise that you liked Finn so much and—'

'Can you just stop talking about it?' I was getting all het up again and I could see that half of the table next to us were straining their nosy ears to hear what was going on.

'I just want you to know how sorry I am.'

'Yep. You've said it now. Let's just leave it, OK?'

He said, 'OK, Faith,' in this tiny little voice and slunk off. I didn't see him again. Good. He should feel bad. He made me feel pretty horrible and he should understand the consequences of his actions.

When we were walking home, Cameron told Megs that the boys are going to the park tomorrow and asked if the girls would come along. Megs agreed with some very enthusiastic head nodding.

Ethan said to me, 'You coming?'

'I don't know. Will Westy be there?'

'I think so, but don't let that stop you. You know that he was just trying to get in on the jokes, don't you? He doesn't always judge things well.'

'Obviously not.'

'Last Sunday night he slept in his uniform because he thought it would save him time in the morning.'

I couldn't help smiling and then Ethan said, 'Go on, come to the park.' And I said yes. I've been thinking about it this evening and I definitely should go. I'll just avoid Westy. Anyway, this outing is not just about boys. I can spend quality time with my besties and breathe the fresh air and enjoy the park. I love the park.

SATURDAY 26TH NOVEMBER

I hate the park. Who thought the park would be a good place to meet? Parks are really only suitable for frolicking about in the sunshine when you can skip about with a Frisbee looking carefree and fanciable. Today was freezing and frosty. Wearing a bobble hat and mittens is not a carefree look. Megs was particularly angry with me for suggesting miniskirts again.

I told her, 'You wouldn't be frozen if you'd chosen something in a practical fabric like corduroy.'

Megs, Lily, Angharad and I got there before the boys so we set up camp on a picnic table near the children's playground.

When the boys arrived there was a bit of an embarrassed silence when Westy threw himself on his knees and said, 'Please forgive me, Faith! Please, oh please.'

I said, 'Westy, you said all that yesterday.'

'I know, but I'm going to have to keep saying it until you forgive me.' And then the idiot actually bowed right down so that his forehead was on the frosty path.

The thing is that overnight I have calmed down a lot. It was a stupid thing to do, but I know that Westy didn't mean to upset me and goodness knows that I've made a few mistakes myself. So I said, 'Oh, all right, I forgive you. Just sit down and be quiet for a bit, will you?'

He looked up with a massive grin and then got up and tried to tiptoe away from me in an inconspicuous fashion. Except Westy isn't very good at inconspicuous, and as he was rounding the end of the table he tripped over Elliot's leg and went flying. Honestly, that boy is such a banana. Ethan pulled Westy up and made him sit down.

To change the subject I started telling them about how they have to help me with the Christmas boxes – and that's when three St Mildred's girls swanned up.

I don't know what it is about the St Minger's girls. I think that when they start at that school they are all fitted with some sort of device that flashes whenever there is a boy within one hundred metres. Wherever there are males those girls just pop up.

Now, you know me, I'm not one to slate other girls, so I'll keep this brief. Their outfits were not what I would call appropriate for icy conditions. These girls seem to have an inability to cover their midriffs so despite the fact the temperature was hovering around zero, two of them were proudly displaying their belly-button rings for everyone to see. If the St Mingers have anything to do with the next stage of evolution, then future generations of girls will be born with a layer of hair around their middles.

One of them sat down next to Elliot. Ang was furious. She eyed the Minger up and down and digging deep to find the tiny bit of herself that isn't an angelic mouse, she came up with the nastiest thing she could think of. She screwed up her face and said, 'Those shoes don't look very practical.' *Ouch.*

You would think that given Ang's scorching comment and the withering stares that the rest of us were giving them (except Lily, she'd been distracted by a crisp packet blowing in the wind) that the St Mildred's girls would have decided it was time to leave, but no. Instead, one of them started telling us about the boob job she was having for her sixteenth birthday.

Ethan said, 'I would have thought you'd have been put off surgery when the work on your face went so disastrously wrong.'

Which reminded me of why I like Ethan.

The Minger looked confused. Eventually she said, 'You're the funny one, are you?' Obviously she's not keen on wit because after that she turned her back on Ethan and spent her time touching Cameron's hair. Megs was not happy.

To show Cameron she didn't care if he wanted to get cosy with another girl, Megs said, 'Oh, Elliot, that's really interesting.'

It's just a shame that it was rather quiet at the time and we all knew that Elliot hadn't said anything.

In the middle of this love-in who should wander past?

Finn.

Finn walking his adorable Labrador puppy.

The cute factor in the park suddenly soared

off the scale and the St Minger's girls started to dribble. They all tried to scramble up at the same time, which led to a tangle of spike heels and hair extensions.

The first one up lunged at the puppy and gushed, 'Gorgeous!'

I'm not sure if she was talking about the dog.

Megs whispered, 'What a mongrel.'

She definitely wasn't talking about the dog.

Finn just smiled at everyone. His sunny, surfer's heart seems to mean that he can't see the bad in anyone. Which is sweet I suppose, but not as funny as when Ethan said, 'You'd better look after your dog, Finn, these girls are looking for some fresh hair extensions.'

One of the Mingers (who apparently was called Cherry – yes, *Cherry*) said, 'You're Finn, right? Hey, you lot should all come to our Christmas Fayre this afternoon.' She said 'you lot' but she was looking at Finn.

Finn shrugged.

Westy said, 'Ladies, if you want to sit on a chubby man's lap you don't need to go to a poxy Christmas Fayre to see Santa, just form an orderly queue.'

Actually, as Cherry explained to us at great length, the fayre was not going to be poxy. It was being opened by a soap star. There was going to be an ice rink and snow machine and a chocolate fountain and a fairground. Westy blushed and Ethan said, 'Is all this so you can raise money for new diamond mobile phone charms?'

Cherry said, 'Actually at St Mildred's we like to give back to the community . . .'

Megs said, 'More like put out to the community.'

'. . . so we're using the funds to help fill Christmas boxes for old people.'

I snuck a look at Finn to see if he was impressed with this combination of cleavage and charity, but it's very hard to read his facial expressions. He was squinting a bit, but that may have been the sun in his eyes.

Westy said, 'Faith's doing that too. She's doing really well.'

Which just goes to show that Ethan is right about Westy's lack of judgement. As if I wanted that girl knowing my business.

Cherry said, 'Yeah? How many boxes you got?'

Westy didn't hesitate. ''Bout five hundred, isn't it, Faith?'

The awful thing was that I could see that Westy was trying to be nice, whereas in actual fact he was just giving me another reason to want to strangle him.

Cherry raised a very plucked eyebrow. She said, 'I bet we get more boxes than you.'

I said, 'It's touching the way you never lose sight of the old people.'

Cherry shook back her hair and looked down her nose at me. 'I can see why you'd be into charity work. You're that girl that got stood up at th—'

Ethan interrupted. 'Faith will beat you.'

Cherry turned on me with a sneer, but before she could say anything else Ethan grabbed my elbow and pulled me up. 'We're going to get a drink,' he said and dragged me away. I hardly had time to be upset by Cherry's remark (although I did manage to squeeze in a quick daydream of her new boobs exploding). I was quite touched that Ethan had stood up for me like that.

We walked to the little café on the other side of the park and Ethan bought me a coffee.

'Don't take any notice,' he said. 'They're just trying to wind you up.'

'It's all right. I've learnt to tune out the squeaky pitch those girls talk at.'

'Girls? I don't really think of them as girls. In my mind they're like those dinosaurs, you know, the ones that walk on their back legs and do that shrill screamy noise and run around taking bites out of other dinosaurs.'

I snorted. 'It must be quite a place in your mind.'

'You should have a look round one day. I'd

probably have to have a bit of a tidy-up first. I wouldn't want you fainting when you saw what I keep in the furthest recesses.'

See, that is what I like about Ethan. He knows how to have a proper nonsense conversation. I thought that we were having a great time, so I was a bit disappointed when he said we should go back. What does that mean? Did he not enjoy talking to me?

We found the others on the swings. The St Mingers had gone and so had Megs. Westy was attempting to use the seesaw as a slide and while everyone was laughing I said to Lily, 'What's happened to Megs?'

'I'm not sure, but she was pulling this face a bit.' Then she pulled Megs's look-at-me-smiling-I'm-not-at-all-about-to-cry face.

I said, 'I'd better be off.'

LATER AGAIN
So I abandoned the laughy good times in the park to go and see what was the matter with Megs.

She opened her front door and said, 'Oh, is that you?'

I said, 'Of course it's me.' And barged my way in.

'I just thought that since I desperately need to talk to you, you might have disappeared off with your fancy man to drink cappuccinos.'

I settled myself on her sofa. 'What is that supposed to mean? I only disappeared off because that annoying girl was going on at me and anyway I thought I'd left you happy enough with your Cameron.'

'He's not my Cameron. He . . . he . . .'

And then she started blubbering, so I was forced to say, 'What's the matter, sweetie? It's all right. You tell me what he's done and I'll sort him out, Megsie.'

'He said . . . he said . . .'

'Yes?'

'He said, "I might go to that Christmas Fayre."'

I was shocked speechless.

'I think he wanted to see that Cherry girl again,' she added.

'What did you say?'

'I said, "Fine".'

'Oh, dear, Megs, boys are not the sensitive, perceptive creatures that girls are. They don't understand the subtleties of human communication. When you say "fine" I am afraid that they are silly enough to think that what you mean is "fine".'

'Really? But I said it in quite a stroppy way.'

'Unfortunately, they are also deaf to tone of voice. He probably thinks you were telling him to go along and have a jolly old time with the Cherry-tart.'

At this point Megs burst into noisy sobs again and I realised that I might need to rethink my plan to make her feel better.

SUNDAY 27TH NOVEMBER

I'm worried about Megs. She is fragile and needs careful handling. I rang her up this morning to help her through her difficult time.

I said, 'Listen you loser, I am out of M&M's. Pick some up and get yourself round here.'

'I haven't got any money and what was the other thing? Oh yes, I am heartbroken and unable to leave my bed of tears.'

'We both know that my bed is much more comfortable than yours—'

'That's because you ruined my mattress the last time you were round here.'

'If your mattress can't take being converted into a bouncy slide then you seriously need to think about upgrading. Anyway, stop your snivelling and listen to me being supportive. You need to come over, so I can sort your life out.'

'Why can't you come round here?'

'I can't be bothered to get out of my PJs.'

LATER

Megs made it eventually, although without the requested sweeties. I was very kind and pointed out that Megs is much more attractive than any St Minger. 'For example,' I told her, 'all of you is real. What with the boobs and the hair extensions and the nails, those girls have barely got any original parts.'

'Also, I'm not a cow.'

'Also, you're not a cow. That was number three on my list.'

'What was number two?'

'You're not named after a fruit or a type of wine.'

'Maybe I should be.'

'Listen, Meggie-poos, I don't think that Cameron is really interested in Cherry-tart at all. Sometimes all that light bouncing off a cleavage just dazzles a boy temporarily. We all know that it's you that Cameron wants.'

'Really?'

'Truly.'

'If you could just get some proof of that, then I'll be perfectly happy again.'

I won't bore you with the details of how that crazy conversation ended. But basically Megs wants me to text Ethan to find out what Cameron is thinking.

As if Ethan and I have a great record when it comes to text messages.

As if our relationship has reached casual texting levels.

And, more to the point, as if boys tell each other what they're thinking.

LATER AGAIN

Granny came round for tea. I asked her, 'Would you text a boy you sort of liked, but weren't sure if he liked you?'

'It's hard for me to answer that question, Faith, because I've never been unsure of any of my gentlemen friends' affection for me.'

Which means Granny has now knocked Icky off the top of my list of outrageously self-confident people.

Maybe I'm worried about looking too keen on Ethan. Actually, I suppose I am keen. I'm just not sure how much he likes me. Which I think is his worst quality. He seems to be all matey and laughs at my jokes, but then sometimes when we're chatting together he just wanders off. I prefer my friends to hang on my every word.

MONDAY 28TH NOVEMBER

Still all quiet at school. No more has been said about the bushes and Ramsbottom hasn't had me arrested yet.

At lunchtime I was wondering what to do about speaking to Ethan, when I got a text from him. He said: **Can I meet you to talk abt Cam and Megan?**

Given everything that has happened, I wasn't sure that sending me a text about meeting up was in very good taste, but at least it seems like he wants to sort out all this nonsense with Megs and Cam too. I didn't want to seem over-enthusiastic to see him so I waited a while and then I replied: **Ok. Where?**

Two minutes later he answered: **Juicy Lucy's at 4?**

So . . . I've sort of got a date to see Ethan. Even if it is to talk about someone else's love life.

LATER

It's not that I don't trust Ethan, and obviously I now know that he had nothing to do with me looking like an idiot at the cinema, but that doesn't mean that I have forgotten how stupid you appear when you hang about waiting for someone. I wanted to leave no room for anyone imagining that I had been stood up again. So, just to be on the safe side, I didn't arrive at Juicy Lucy's until quarter past four and secondly, I took along a little something to stop me looking lonely if Ethan didn't show – Angharad.

When we got there Ethan was sitting by the door looking worried. He said, 'I thought you weren't coming.'

I couldn't resist smiling at him because he really did look quite pleased to see me.

I gave Angharad a look to let her know it was time to go.

She took a deep breath and said in a stilted voice, 'I just came in for a takeaway milkshake.' Then she walked towards the counter like she had a rod up her back. Good grief. In the film of my life I won't be letting any of my friends play themselves. I'd just sat down when Ang popped back again and said in a loud whisper, 'Actually, Faith, I don't think I've got enough money for a milkshake, so is it OK if I just pretend my mum wants me to go home?'

Peering through my hands, which I had spread across my face to cover my fast-rising blush, I said, 'Yes. Great. You do that. Lovely. Thanks for your discretion, Ang.'

Ethan was cracking up.

When Angharad had bumbled off and Ethan had stopped smirking he said, 'Thanks for coming.'

I said, 'Well, I had to do something about Megan.'

'She's got Cameron worked up. He says she's gone all funny and hasn't answered his text.'

'What did he say?'

'"What's the matter?"'

I sighed. 'That's the wrong question.'

'How is it the wrong question? He wants to know why Megan is acting all weird, so he asked her.'

'He's not supposed to ask. He's supposed to know.'

'What if he doesn't?'

I felt a bit drained at this point. Explaining how to be human to boys is very tiring.

Ethan went on, 'Listen, Cam isn't very good at communication, but I know that he really likes Megan. I, as you know, am gifted at talking and also really quite intelligent. Why don't you explain it to me and then I'll see if I can make it clear to Cameron by comparing the situation to a football game. Or by beating him over the head with a stick.'

'Cameron was keen on going to the St Mildred's Christmas Fayre.'

He looked at me for a minute. Then he said slowly, 'Is this about that plastic girl with the disappearing skirt? What was her name, Sherry?'

I nodded my head.

'*Really?*'

'He was gawping at her a bit.'

'People gawp at woodland animals that have been run over. It's not because they like what they see.'

'So he doesn't like her?'

'Cameron likes Megan. Everybody knows that.'

'He just needs to persuade Megs.'

'Why don't we all go bowling on Saturday? You ask your lot and I'll get Cam, Elliot and Westy . . . Er, do you mind Westy being there?'

Strangely, I didn't really mind.

'Just tell him not to try any more tricks on me,' I said.

'I will. I really think that if Cameron and Megan spend some time together they'll sort it out.'

For a boy, it was quite a good plan.

While we were talking it over we had smoothies and at one point (when I was telling him about sticking false eyebrows on all the safety glasses in Mrs Macready's room), Ethan laughed so hard that fruit pulp came out of his nose.

Given that two weeks ago I swore I would hate him forever, I had a pretty good time.

TUESDAY 29TH NOVEMBER

I've spent so much time on Megan's love life recently that I've not given enough thought to trying to beat the St Mingers (I mean, doing my bit for charity and helping the old people). I made the girls come round with me at lunchtime today to get some more volunteers. We got one Year Eight (I think she agreed so that we'd talk to her for a while, she seemed a bit friendless), plus Zoe's sister and a group of Year Sevens.

I think the Year Sevens were scared of Lily. I may or may not have given them the impression that Lily can be violent when she's angry. And I may or may not have suggested that indifference to old people is what really angers her.

It's all in a good cause though, isn't it?

Showing the St Mingers who's boss.

WEDNESDAY 30TH NOVEMBER

After school I demonstrated how selfless I am once again, by braving the cold weather and going shopping for old-people gifts with Megs, Lily and Angharad. I took them to the pound shop and said, 'Imagine you're an old person. Now pile the things you would like for Christmas in the basket.'

We ended up with a tin of boiled sweets, hair dye, extra-strong support tights, chocolate coins, mouthwash and a large print crossword book.

I'm not sure who chose the exploding bangers and the satin boxer shorts, but I put them back. Lily chose a huge blister pack of bubble gum balls, but she'd eaten most of them by the time we'd got to the checkout, so I didn't worry about it too much.

On the way home I saw Finn walking his puppy. He was on the other side of the roundabout to me so there wasn't much opportunity for a chat. I jumped up and down and shrieked 'FINN!' for a bit and when he'd finally noticed me he gave me quite an enthusiastic wave. That's a good sign, isn't it?

DECEMBER

THURSDAY 1ST DECEMBER

I woke up this morning to find an elderly man in my bedroom. He claimed to be my father but it still gave me a nasty turn.

He said, 'Faith, have you looked out your window?'

Had I looked out of my window? Oh, yes, when I am awoken at the unnecessary time of seven a.m. by a man who frankly ought to spend his mornings trying to spread his hair evenly over his shiny head, my first thought is to leap from my cosy nest and check that all is well with the world outside by peering out the window and perhaps throwing a cheery wave to those like-minded types who are also awake at such an unnatural time. This is what I was thinking, but luckily for my doddering father I was trying to remain mostly asleep so I only said, 'No.'

'It's snowing!'

Well, that was good news, but really a reason to burrow further into the duvet, not to linger at windows and other draughty areas.

'Brilliant. Wake me at ten with a full English.' I pulled the covers over my head.

He said, 'Faith, Just because it's snowing it doesn't mean you automatically get a day off.'

Good grief. I have told him about this. I really am quite good at tuning out his mindless babbling when it could interfere with important activities like sleeping, makeup application or looking attractive whilst sitting in his rusty car, but how can I be expected to ignore his raving when he says something as stupid as this?

So I said politely but firmly, 'Yes it does, you pillock.' I pulled the covers over my head again.

'It's really not that deep. I'm sure school will expect you to manage a little snow in pursuit of your education.'

'Dad, you adults make these crazy rules for yourself about perseverance and never taking time off to watch antiques shows in your jammies, but there are a group of grown-ups who are smarter than the rest of you. They call them teachers. They fancy a long summer holiday, so they have one. If you ask them why they say, "It is for the children – they really need a break." They don't want to work the ridiculously long hours that you choose to, so they finish at three. If you ask them why they say, "It is for the children – their poor brains cannot cope with a long day."'

Dad was twitching.

'And if it snows they do not fancy getting their feet cold, so they close the school. If you ask them why they say, "It is for the poor children – they must not get their feet cold."'

'Yes, well, can't say I'm regretting not entering

the teaching profession if you're an example of the modern pupil. Anyway, until we hear otherwise you need to get ready for school.'

I barely had time for an eye-roll before Mum wafted in.

'Faith, the radio says your school is closed.'

'Better make it half ten, Dad,' I said and snuggled down.

LATER
I've had a super day. People would be so much happier if they weren't separated from their duvets in winter. I've tried to reassure Dad that I won't have missed anything today. Most of the teachers are handing out the Christmas word searches already. Hope school is closed tomorrow.

FRIDAY 2ND DECEMBER
School is not closed. I am attempting to put my coat on over my duvet.

LATER
Didn't quite manage to get the duvet under my coat, so I decided on the battered, floor-length fake-fur coat that hangs about like a dead bear in the cupboard under the stairs. It smells a bit musty, but it is very warm.

Miss Ramsbottom was not keen and started

ribbiting on about uniform, but I said firmly but politely, 'Miss R, I am an eco-warrior. I've got a family of badgers sheltering under here. Please don't hate the animals.'

I am such a nice person that despite the treacherous snowy conditions I actually waited at school until the end of choir rehearsal and tolerated Icky flouncing past me and saying, 'Poodle boy keeping you waiting again?' just so I could generate more support for the Christmas boxes.

I gathered together as many people from the rehearsal as possible in Juicy Lucy's and told them what it was about. Once again the miserable monkeys started whining on about lack of money and fear of old people. So I decided to cut to the chase, I said firmly but politely, 'Shut up, you cretins. Who is going to sign up?'

Deathly silence.

Then Ethan said, 'I'll do one.'

And Westy said, 'I'll do ten.'

It's nice that he's still trying to make things up to me, but I'm not sure he can be trusted to gather suitable gifts for pensioners. This is the boy who told us that last Christmas he removed a packet of rubber gloves from under the sink at home to give to his own mother. Ethan said he would supervise Westy. Counting them as two boxes, my grand total so far is fourteen boxes. Lame.

Most people had shuffled off and I was left staring into my milkshake when Ethan came over.

He said, 'Can I make a suggestion about your Christmas boxes?'

I raised my eyebrows. I don't know where I am with Ethan. I kind of like him, but I feel like I made an idiot of myself assuming that he was the one pretending to be Finn. Sometimes I wonder if Ethan is laughing at me.

He said, 'You need to sell it to people.'

'The whole idea is that people are supposed to be volunteering to do this. You know, giving their time and effort for nothing, to help the old dearies.'

'You need to sex it up a bit.'

'Oh, gross. Listen, I've seen what's under my granny's skirt and it only gets worse above the pop socks.'

'Not the geriatrics. Appeal to the girls with the boys, and the boys with the girls. Have a joint meeting to wrap the boxes and then we can all go off together to deliver them. No one can resist the opportunity to meet the opposite sex. That's how we all ended up in this choir disaster, isn't it?'

'I'll have you know that I've got a fine ear for music.'

'You might have a fine ear for music, but you haven't got a fine gob for it.'

I whacked him over the head for that. It was just like old times.

It is quite a good idea. I am going to ask if we can use the hall at school. Ethan said if I make a poster that he would put it up at the boys' school.

SATURDAY 3RD DECEMBER

Freezing day with sleet in the wind. Not good conditions for keeping my nose un-red and fanciable. I put on a layer of foundation, two layers of powder, then wrapped my conk in a scarf and hoped for the best. I did consider Sam's balaclava, but it would have messed up my hair. I could have chopped a hole in the top, but I thought then my head would look like when you grow cress out of the top of an eggshell.

I went into town to meet Megs before the Big Bowling Date. I was early, so I thought I'd help Mum with her Christmas shopping (by making a list of things she really must buy me) when the shadow of something tall and jangly loomed over the rack of earrings I was admiring.

I said, 'Hello, Cherry. I see you're dressed for the weather.'

She was wearing thigh-length fur boots.

She said, 'Hello, Hope. Is that fit boy with you?' She looked about like Finn might be hiding in the rings display.

'I expect I'll see him later.'

'We had a lovely time with him at the Christmas Fayre.'

My mouth dropped open at this. Finn went to their stupid fayre? Why didn't I know this?

'You can tell him we raised loads of money.' She scratched her eyebrow with one of her talon nails. 'Yeah, loads of money for our Christmas boxes,' she continued. 'How many boxes have you got, Hope?'

Instead of answering, I "accidentally" jogged her and she skewered her own eyeball with her dagger-nail. While she was trying to mop up the river of mascara running down her face Megs appeared. She twirled round to show me her outfit (covered by a gigantic coat) and said, 'Do they do kitten-heeled bowling shoes? I need a bit of height.'

After we'd bid a friendly goodbye to Cherry ('Bye, Cherry. Hope your school burns down and your leg extensions drop off ...') we went to do some real shopping.

The problem with shops is that they're not organised to suit me. It would be much more helpful if they could sort out the things that are a) in my size and b) not ugly, and put them in a roped-off area for me. I did ask Megs if she'd like to be my personal shopper, but she shook her head.

'Faith, I don't fall for your offers of employment.

Remember when we started in Year Seven and you talked our Maths table into being your personal assistants for a week?'

'Oh, yes, that was a good week. I was freed from the weight of carrying my own bag and the toil of sharpening my own pencils.'

'Yeah, because by "personal assistant" you meant slaves. And I was the only one you didn't bamboozle into it. And you said that was when you decided to be my friend, because I was the only one who had any backbone.'

'Yep, I really respected that backbone. Me getting friendly had nothing to do with the fact that you were writing your party invitations at the time.'

And Megs beat me over the head with the pair of jeans she was holding.

I said, 'See? We're a perfect combination. I'm devastatingly attractive and able to wangle party invitations and you can fashion a weapon from fashion. Stick with me, Megsie, and we'll go far.'

Megs was about to lay in with a double attack using both the jeans and a fluffy jacket when a shop assistant asked if we were planning to buy either of the items. So we decided to leave in a dignified manner (i.e. snorting with laughter and jabbing each other in the ribs).

Outside the shop Megs said, 'No, but really,

apart from your laziness, rudeness and constant demands for sweeties, you are quite a good friend.'

'Stop, Megs, before I'm overcome with all your kind words. Oh, no, wait, there were only six them. Have you not read that lists of acceptable compliments I gave you?'

'Shut up! I'm trying to tell you that you're really nice for setting up this thing with Cameron.'

'Well, I couldn't let you go around running your own life, could I?'

Then we had a hug and started off for the bowling alley.

We'd got most of the way there before Megs realised that I'd used her cuddle as an opportunity to nab the Mars bar that was in her pocket.

LATER

When we got there things were a little bit awkward. Megs barely said hello to Cameron, I still feel a bit weird around Westy, and Lily was transfixed by the ball polisher. Angharad managed to say to Elliot, 'Are those new shoelaces?' and that was the extent of our conversation for five minutes.

The boys were no help. They were mostly whacking each other over the head and telling anyone who'd listen how brilliant they are at bowling, but none of them seemed particularly keen to get started. In the end it was Westy who got things going. He picked up a ball and rubbed it on his trousers like cricketers do. He turned to us and winked and took these long, crouching steps backwards (until he bumped into a waitress) then he ran forward right up on his tippy-toes. As he got close to the line he swung the ball backwards really hard and then lunged forward. The ball went flying down the lane.

And Westy went with it.

Angharad was the first one to stop crying with laughter, so she went to help Westy, who had got his sausage fingers stuck in the holes in the ball. He said, 'Did you see that? Did you see how straight I got it? If I hadn't've gone with it I reckon that would have been a strike. I should get the points for that.' He looked right at me and I think that's probably when I completely forgave him. Nobody could believe that Westy ever meant any harm. The great haddock.

After that things were a bit more relaxed.

When it was my turn to bowl, I was a bit nervous. It's not a very flattering sport and I started to wish I'd worn more substantial knickers. I managed to keep my behind under control and didn't do anything too embarrassing (unlike Lily, who bowled down the wrong lane).

When I sat down, Cameron said to me, 'What shall I do?'

I'm not sure that I know him well enough for life guidance, but I did my best and said, 'Follow your dreams and stay away from hard drugs.'

He looked at me like my name was Insanie McMental and then said very slowly, 'I meant what shall I do about Megan?'

'Oh. Chat to her. Talk about something she's interested in. Maybe try a romantic gesture.'

He nodded and turned back to Megs and said, 'Did you see the football last night, Megan? And do you want a Coke?'

Megan obviously doesn't have my high standards of romance because the next time I looked round the pair of them were having a tickle fight.

And we all know what that means.

When it was Angharad's go she picked up a little pink ball and held it against her chest with both hands.

Westy said, 'Shall we put the kiddie rails up for you, Angharad?'

Ang took a dainty little run-up and swung the ball down the lane. It zoomed straight down the middle and smashed into the centre pin sending all the others flying. We gave her a round of applause for her beginner's luck and then ... she did it again. Turns out that Angharad is a tiny bowling powerhouse.

While I was watching Megs and Cam getting more and more silly, Ethan sat down next to me and said, 'We're pretty good at bringing people together. Maybe we should charge.'

I said, 'Obviously, I'd get most of the money since I'm the brains.'

'Obviously.' He turned round to look at Angharad and Elliot, who were comparing key rings. 'Do you think we should help them out next?'

'I think they're already having more fun than they can handle by talking about Ang's stick insect and Elliot's paper round. I don't think they'll ever get to snogging unless we draw them a diagram.'

'Elliot does like a good diagram.' He smiled his sparkly smile at me again. 'What about you, Faith? What do you like?'

I went a bit goosepimply when he said my name. 'Oh, you know. The small things in life. Chocolate buttons, lollipops . . . diamond earrings.'

He laughed. 'You seem a bit distracted today. Are you all right?'

Of all the conversations with a boy that I have rehearsed in my head, not once have I imagined that one would be asking me seriously how I was. I said, 'Fine.' In an unconvincing way.

He went on looking at me. I couldn't tell him that I was feeling left out of all this coupling-up business. And I certainly couldn't tell him that I was trying to decide if I like him as much as Finn. What I needed was a neutral topic that didn't give away too much about me. Before I could think of one of those I blurted out, 'I'm really scared I'm going to be excluded for driving Miss Ramsbottom's car.'

'Ah.'

Which made me think that the next time a boy asks me if I am all right I will be more forceful about saying, 'Fine'.

But then he said, 'It's tough when your imagination carries you away and before you know it you've landed yourself in trouble, isn't it?'

'Yes. People keep telling me I ought to grow up and think about the consequences of my actions, but—'

'The consequences keep pretty quiet when a funny idea pops in your head?'

'Exactly. And who am I to silence the comedy genius within me? How do you know all this?'

'I know I give the impression of being a sophisticated and controlled young man, but I've actually got myself into a few situations too.'

'Really?'

'Really. Last year I subscribed the head of Maths to a rather naughty magazine and had them sent to the school.'

'What happened?'

'They rang my parents. I was grounded. There was a huge row.'

'That's what's going to happen to me. I just know it.'

'Listen, Faith, firstly, you haven't been caught yet so maybe you—'

'Oh no, you're not going to suggest confessing, are you?'

'What? Are you insane? Never confess. The way I see it is that you can square it with the universe by saying, "I know that was a really dumb thing to do and I have learnt my lesson. I will never drive a teacher's car again". That way fate knows it's not necessary for you to be found out.'

My eyes had gone quite wide by this point. I said, 'You've really thought about this, haven't you?'

He nodded.

'Man, you must have done some naughty stuff.'

He tried to look sheepish, but he actually looked a little bit proud. He said, 'Yeah, but never the same thing twice.'

I shook my head.

'Look, don't worry. I think it'll all be OK. And if you do get found out, don't panic, you're not a bad person, Faith. People would get over it eventually.'

Then he quite tactfully started telling me about when he was at primary school with Westy and they were in the nativity play. Ethan was stuck at the back as one of many shepherds, but Westy insisted on being an angel. He wore a white duvet cover and carried a wand. When another kid stole his line Westy wrestled them to the ground, waved his wand and said, 'I'm going to turn you into a frog.' I laughed so hard that I had to cheer up a bit. I also felt quite reassured by what Ethan said. It will all be all right in the end.

By the time we left, Megs and Cameron were holding hands and Angharad had the highest score by a mile. When she made her gazillionth strike I heard Elliot say, 'What a woman!'

Which was both true and very funny.

Cameron's dad was waiting to give Cam and Ethan a lift. Cameron gave Megs this little squeezy hug before they went.

I had a strange thought that I'd quite like a squeeze from Ethan, but he just said, 'Better not jingle those car keys near Faith, Mr H,' which made Megs snort with laughter.

I got the bus back with Lily. I was pleased that we'd managed to get Megs and Cameron together, but somehow it had left me feeling a bit flat.

Lily said, 'What's the matter, Faith? You look like my cat did that time I forgot her birthday.'

I didn't want to hear any more of that story so I launched into a lengthy explanation of how my delicate emotional balance has been thrown out by the recent turbulent events and the insensitivity of others in forming happy relationships.

I said, 'I'm fed up.'

Lily patted me on the arm and beamed at me. 'When I'm fed up I think about crunchy peanut butter on toast and new trainers. The world is a wonderful place and I really can't think of a single problem . . .'

And that's when I told her she was still wearing her bowling shoes.

SUNDAY 4TH DECEMBER

Megs rang me way too early this morning. She said, 'Get your Nike miniskirt on. We're going to watch some football.'

'It's practically snowing. The only thing that I'll be wearing this morning is my duvet.'

'Cameron's going to be there.'

'You won't want me there then, I'd only get in the way of your special squeezes.'

'I'll want you there while he's doing the footballing bit, otherwise I'll have no one to talk to.'

'Oh, I see, and then what am I supposed to do when you two are getting cosy?'

'You could take an interest in the scenery.'

I growled.

'Or you could talk to Finn. Who, I'm sure you remember, is also on the team. And who, I've been meaning to say, is always looking at you.'

'Really?'

'Really. I'll meet you at the park.'

So somehow I found myself spending my Sunday morning watching teenage boys kicking about in the mud. It wasn't much fun to start with because, despite my frozen, but glamorous good looks, not one of them glanced in my direction. All their attention was on the stupid ball. And that's why I have never liked football.

Eventually, they stopped playing and Cameron came jogging over. Megs started gushing like he'd just invented lip-gloss or done something else actually worthwhile rather than run backwards and forwards on a muddy field. I thought now was probably the time for me to take an interest in the scenery, so I headed in the direction of the best view, which happened to be of Finn's legs in shorts.

I said, 'Oh, hi Finn, I didn't know you played on the same team as Cameron.'

'Really? I thought you asked me if I did at Ryan's party.' He wrinkled his super-cute nose up. 'Three times.'

I tried to gloss over things with a light-hearted laugh, but it sounded more like a choking hyena. Then I said, 'Oh. Yeah. That's right. I remember now.'

'Do you forget the things that you've said too? I do that. My mum's like, "You said you wanted picking up at four," and I'm like, "Did I?"'

Then we had a nice chuckle about how forgetful the pair of us are.

I asked him how the footballing was.

'Well, we've been pretty narrow in the midfield.'

I didn't know if this was a good or bad thing so I nodded my head thoughtfully.

'And most of the play has been long-ball stuff.'

He seemed to be expecting me to respond so I said, 'That's nice. No one wants little balls, do they?'

As soon as I said it I cringed. Finn just blinked at me and then, fortunately, someone blew a whistle and apparently that meant that they were going to play some more. I couldn't really see what for. I thought the first forty-five minutes had pretty much covered everything. So Finn gave me one more lovely (if slightly confused) smile and jogged off. I did manage to speak to him again at the end and to invite him to come to the Christmas box meeting. If only the morning had taken place somewhere warm it might have all been worth it.

MONDAY 5TH DECEMBER

Mrs Webber has sorted it so that we can use the school hall for the box meeting after school on Thursday. She has even agreed to store the boxes in her cupboard till Saturday, when she will come into school especially to supervise us collecting the boxes before delivering them. I did suggest that supervision wasn't necessary, but she looked at me and said, 'Faith, you're helping the aged. That's one miracle. If I expect to leave you unsupervised with a load of boys without trouble that would be asking for two miracles and Santa Claus doesn't like us to be greedy, so I will be there on both Thursday and Saturday and I will organise tea and biscuits.'

She's not a bad old thing. I said, 'Mrs Webber, you're not a bad old thing. Perhaps you would like one of our Christmas boxes for the elderly?'

And she just said, 'Get away with you.' Which is what adults say when they think you're being quite funny, but they don't want you to get cocky.

It's all quite short notice, but I have put up loads of posters and Megs got me Ethan's email address from Cameron, so I have emailed him a poster to put up in his school. Fingers crossed that plenty of boys turn up.

TUESDAY 6TH DECEMBER
Cameron has texted Megs to ask if he can sit next to her at the box meeting. Megs is quite pleased.

In fact, she's been discussing colours for bridesmaids' dresses.

WEDNESDAY 7TH DECEMBER

Dragged round to Granny's house for tea. I had a stomach ache so I asked to be left at home, but Dad said, 'We'll all have a stomach ache by the time we get home so it doesn't make much difference.'

While we were there I made the mistake of mentioning the Christmas box meeting tomorrow, thinking that Granny would be impressed with how organised I am; instead she said, 'What time is the meeting?'

This question made me feel sicker than the flabby vegetable lasagna Granny had just served us.

'Why do you want to know what time it is?' I squeaked.

'So that I'm not late, silly.'

I tried desperately to explain that there was no need for Granny to attend, but she is adamant that we will require her help.

Now both Mrs Webber and Granny will be at the meeting ready to hamper my attempts to get friendly with Finn. Maybe it will work out OK, sometimes two ancient people are better than one because they distract each other by talking about the weather and how everyone under twenty-one should be whipped and sent to bed without any supper.

As usual, on the way back from Granny's we

were expected to get excited about a trip to the nearby twenty-four-hour Tesco. Sam and I had abandoned Mum and Dad, and then I spotted a packet of frozen peas that had burst open so we were having a friendly pea fight, when who should float down the aisle? Finn. It's almost as if my thinking about how to charm him at the meeting had conjured him up. I can't think of another good reason for him being there. I'm wondering now if perhaps he wandered in by mistake.

He said, 'Hey, Faith.' As if he wasn't surprised to see me or the peas in my hair at all.

'Hello, Finn.'

He looked at Sam. 'Hey, little dude.'

Sam said, 'My name's Sam. Are you the one she fan—'

He didn't get to finish that sentence because I whacked him over the head with a box of frozen fish.

'Whoa, Faith! Hey listen . . .' Finn leant towards me and for a moment I thought he was going to tell me how attractive he found me, but instead he said, 'Make sure you get the dolphin-friendly tuna.'

'Um. OK.'

'Because dolphins are cool.'

Sam started laughing. 'Yes, Faith, dolphins are cool and save the rainforests and—'

I smacked him again.

Finn squinted at me. I hoped he didn't think I was a violent person.

He said, 'About this box thing.'

'What box thing?'

'Christmas boxes? You said there was a meeting? So, are you, like, collecting boxes for old people or something? Shall I bring you some boxes?'

Sam said, 'I think flowers are more traditional than boxes.' And he started flicking peas at me again.

I said, 'We do need boxes. Shoeboxes are best . . .'

'Do the grannies love boxes then? Crazy.'

'Well, we put some presents in the boxes.'

'Really?'

'Yes. Really.'

A pea bounced off my head and hit Finn's shoe. He picked it up and handed it back to Sam. There was a long pause while Sam looked between the two of us and I tried to discreetly stamp on his toe.

Finn was quite happily admiring the range of frozen chips.

I said, 'Soooo . . . I'll see you at the meeting?'

'Yeah, sure. I'll bring some shoes. See you later, Faith.' And he wandered off to the pet aisle.

All in all it was a bit of an odd encounter.

LATER

He seems to like animals.

That's nice. Shows a caring nature.

I like animals.

As long as they don't moult, dribble or bite.

LATER STILL

I'm worried about tomorrow. My stomach ache has got worse. It's probably a stress ulcer.

THURSDAY 8TH DECEMBER

In some ways the box meeting went very well. In other ways less well.

I thought that Granny had already shown me what embarrassment was that time she took me nightdress shopping with her and kept grabbing old men to ask them if they preferred stretch satin or winceyette, but she's taken me to new depths today. It started off pretty well (mostly because Granny was late and Mrs Webber was keeping a low profile behind her tea table). Tons of people showed up from all years of our school and the boys' school. Although not all of them brought boxes with them. Cheek. What do they think this is? A dating agency? I sent them to the corner shop; I said the minimum entry requirement was a box of Matchmakers.

Then Granny decided to perk us all up by

arriving wearing what looked like a run-over squirrel as a hat. Just in case there were a few people who hadn't noticed her (like the blind and a couple of emo girls who had those hoodies that zip right over your heads) she bellowed to me across the hall, 'Faith, are you going to introduce me to your friends?'

I scooted over to her quickly and said, 'Sorry, Granny, it would take too long to tell you the name of everyone in this hall.' Ha. I thought that would show her that she's not the only popular one. And she looked almost impressed until one of the Tarty Party came stropping past in a cloud of pound-shop body spray and said to me, 'Urg, what are you doing here?'

Granny gave me a piercing look. I tried to give her one back, but to be honest I think the sharpness of her nose gives her an unfair advantage.

'I'll just assist where I'm most needed, shall I?' she said. Before I had time to answer she'd decided that the people who most needed her help were a group of boys. And conveniently one of the boys was being dropped off by his beardy granddad. In fact it was the granddad that Granny seemed to be 'helping' the most. Honestly, some people think of nothing but boys. I, on the other hand, was completely focused on getting the boxes wrapped (with just half an eye on the door waiting for Finn to turn up).

Some people's wrapping was a bit sketchy. Good job we'd brought along a load of cheap-but-cheerful paper. Elliot, it turns out, has hidden gift-presentation talents. He soon had the girls flocking around him saying things like, 'Do mine, Elliot,' and, 'How do you get your corners so smooth, Elliot?' Angharad (who had come over a bit pale when she saw Granny's squirrel-torture hat) had cheered right up and was stood next to him looking very proud. When he asked her to curl some ribbon for him I thought she was going to cry with happiness. I didn't get to watch the sweet but incredibly slow unfolding of their lurve for long though, I had to go and persuade Westy that a spud gun wasn't a suitable present for a pensioner. It is exhausting being the responsible one, but someone had to do it. Mrs Webber seemed to have nodded off behind the tea table. (Why are teachers always so tired? It's not like they've got a proper job.) And Granny certainly wasn't thinking about the safety of old people. In fact I'm pretty sure she was thinking about the snogging of old people. One with a beard in particular. *Ew* gross. I have almost put myself off my late-night snack of the chocolate tree decorations that I found hanging around somewhere. (Actually, they were hanging around on the tree, but I've only taken the ones from the back.)

So with Webber snoozing and Granny schmoozing it was left to me to go round checking everyone else's boxes. I also asked people to write a Christmas card to pop in too. You know what old people are like about cards; they like them as much as a proper present.

I was admiring Ethan and Westy's boxes when Granny finally remembered that she wasn't there to flirt and came to stick her nose in. My stomach was aching a bit again so I'd just sat down when she swooped in on me. I had been hoping that my illness was making me look sort of pale and interesting, but Granny said, 'Why are you wincing like an old man trying to get his socks on?'

Westy sniggered.

'Have you got a tummy ache?' Granny went on.

I said, 'No, I'm fine.' But it was too late.

'Are your pants too tight?'

That made Westy double up laughing.

'Is the pain on one side?'

I wanted to tell her that the pain was in my bottom and that she was it, but I settled for trying to distract her by saying, 'Look! Isn't that an old man with a large moustache over there?'

'Because if it's on the left it might be appendicitis. Although we thought you had appendicitis a couple of Christmases ago, didn't we? But that turned out to be trapped—'

She didn't get to say 'wind' because I pulled her hat over her mouth and said, 'You mustn't catch cold, Granny.'

There was a bit of a pause while we all watched Granny extract squirrel tail from her nose. I will say this for my granny, she has got some class. She pushed back her hat like she was a film star and said, 'Do you know what would be nice?' like nothing had happened. 'It would be nice to have a spot of music.'

Westy, bless him, behaved as if he chats with mad old grannies every day of the week. He said, 'Yeah, I like to listen to music when I've got to do difficult stuff like wrapping presents or Maths homework or sitting still. Do you like thrash metal, Mrs Faith's Gran?'

'Is that one of the shouting ones?' Granny asked.

'Yeah, like this.' And Westy stood up and gave us a burst of one of his favourites along with some air guitar.

Granny beamed at him, which just goes to show that she had taken a shine to him because if I so much as whistle she clutches her ears and reminds me that my primary school Music teacher put me in the 'listeners'' group for a reason.

'Well it's very energetic, isn't it?' Granny said. Then she started wittering on about the ancient music that she likes to listen to. 'And you should see me do the twist, young man,' she said to Westy.

'Is that that crazy dancing?' Westy asked.

So Granny treated us to a one-woman demonstration of how old people used to dance before they had music videos to teach them how to do it properly. She stuck out her elbows and jerked about. If I hadn't known better I would have thought she was being electrocuted by the Christmas tree lights. Westy, on the other hand, seemed delighted. But then Westy is delighted by pictures of animals in hats. I was worried that Granny's bones would snap, but Westy actually started twisting about with her. I wished I could climb into a Christmas box. Clearly what Granny needed to keep her busy was something to criticise, so I sent her over to the Tarty Party table to tell them where they were going wrong with their hair and makeup.

'Wow,' Ethan said, 'your gran—'

'Is crazy?' I suggested. 'Is obviously determined to embarrass the hell out of me?'

'I was going to say "reminds me of you", but I'm sensing that that's not what you want to hear right now.'

'No, I don't want to hear it now. Or ever.'

'Listen, Faith, before I annoy you by comparing you to a fun and vivacious old lady, I wanted to talk to you . . .'

I was trying to work out whether being compared to Granny was OK if it made me fun and vivacious, so it took me a minute to realise that Ethan had trailed off.

He started again. 'There's something—'

Then I heard a 'Hey, Faith,' behind me. It was Finn. With a large box. He grinned his big lazy grin at me and Ethan.

Ethan looked from Finn to me and said, 'Well, it's only a matter of time before Lily gets her hair tangled up in the sellotape. I might just go and help her out with that.' And he disappeared. Leaving me alone with Finn.

Finn's attention seemed to have drifted off, but then he said, 'Big crowd.' And he admired the chaos for a bit.

I, on the other hand, admired his cheekbones, or at least I did until I realised what I was doing and then I blushed and admired my shoes until the silence had gone on too long and I was forced to say, 'What's in the box?'

'Oh. Yeah. My dad works at this place and he said that maybe you would like these for your Christmas old people thing.' He opened up the box.

It was full of individually-wrapped scented soaps. His dad is a manager at the Apple Blossom toiletries warehouse. The soaps are seconds because the labels have been stuck on a bit wonky, but I doubt the elderly are going to notice that. They'll be in lavender-scented heaven.

I said, 'That's amazing. Thank you so much.'

Then I saw Granny heading towards us. My granny was about to meet Finn. And probably say something. It was unlikely to be a good something that made me sound like the kind of cool girl that Finn should think about dating. I panicked. I looked around the hall desperately for Megs. When I caught her eye I tried to mime: *Granny alert! Granny approaching fit boy of my dreams. Help me!* Only, obviously I didn't want Finn to know that there was anything strange going on so I attempted to act it out using only my eyebrows and a touch of my left ear. Fortunately, Megs strained what little brains she has and managed to get the general gist. She whizzed across the room, took Finn by the elbow (I'm a bit jealous of that part, imagine what it would be like to touch his elbow . . .) and steered him off to look at her selection of gift tags. And I was left with Granny to hand out the soap.

There was enough soap to put one in every single box. All eighty-seven of them. They wouldn't all fit in Mrs Webber's cupboard so we stacked some of them under her desk. Then Mrs Webber snorted back into life (I can only imagine that Mr Webber is a man with a very strong stomach if that's what he has to deal with before breakfast every morning) and she said that I'd better make a speech.

I said, 'What? Talk in front of all these people?'

Mrs Webber said, 'Faith, I've seen you shout across a lunch room with three hundred girls in to tell Megan you've got something stuck in your toenail. I'm sure you can manage to tell your friends when you're next meeting to hand out these boxes.'

'Couldn't you do it? You're a teacher so you've had the part of your brain that gets embarrassed removed, haven't you? Otherwise you wouldn't be wearing those shoes.'

'Just get on with it, Faith.'

She is such a mean old boot. Why can't people with naturally foghorny voices and no shame help out shy and gentle types like myself?

I stood up on a chair and said, 'Shut up, you turnips! Thank you all for coming today and bringing all these super things for the lovely oldies. You've done a really good job. We're going to be handing out these boxes at the old people's home on Saturday morning so if you'd like to spend some more time chatting up the opposite sex . . . ahem, I mean making the elderly happy then you need to be here, in the hall again, at exactly ten o'clock.'

At the end Mrs W chimed in and said, 'Let's thank Faith for all her work in organising this.'

And everybody gave me a round of applause. It

was lovely. As you know, Mrs Webber has always been my favourite teacher.

Granny had to rush off to get ready for a date (she'd only left three hours to put on her makeup, which I think was cutting it a bit fine) so Megs and I had to get a lift home with Dad. While we were waiting outside for him to pick us up, Finn strolled past.

He said, 'So, like, what day was it again that we're delivering these boxes?'

'Saturday.'

'Cool. I'll be there.' And he sauntered off.

I squeezed Megs's hand and said in a very discreet, low voice because he might still be able to hear us, 'Oh. My. Goodness. That is practically a date.'

'If it is, you should stop talking in that Mr Hampton voice. I don't think Finn is into creepy Science teachers.'

I can't wait for Saturday.

When Dad finally turned up several minutes late he asked if I'd had a good time with Granny at the box meeting.

I gave him a death stare. 'Have you ever had a good time with Granny? Anywhere? Ever?'

'Oh dear, bit embarrassing, was she?'

'She danced.'

'I see.'

'She sang.'

Dad had the decency to suck in his breath at this point.

'She told several people that they're too fat. And . . .' I was wincing at the memory, '. . . I think she was trying to chat up one of my friends.'

Dad shook his head. 'Do you know, Faith, you've just described the way she behaved at my wedding.' He sighed. 'At least you haven't got two albums of photos to remind you of the happy day.'

'No, but Westy's friend has already put her bone-crunching "dancing" on the internet.'

FRIDAY 9TH DECEMBER

Miss Ramsbottom hauled me into her office for another little chat today. My heart sank into my socks because I thought the car thing was finally coming out. I kept repeating what Ethan had said to me: *They'll get over it*. But it turns out that for once Ramsbottom was not angry with me. Although, it's hardly surprising that I hadn't guessed this because it seems that her not-angry face is pretty much the same as her angry face (bloodless and haughty). Still, there was no mistaking the ringing praise in her words. 'It seems you have avoided trouble this week.'

I was so overcome by this demonstration of

emotion from Miss Ramsbottom that all I could manage was a small choking noise.

'I'm glad to see you taking an interest in the community and Mrs Webber says that you have fitted into your new tutor group well.'

Good old Webber.

'Miss Ramsbottom, does this mean that I can go back to my old tutor group next term?'

'I think we'd best wait till January to review your progress. But I wanted to encourage you to keep up the good work.'

Which I took as a definite 'yes' for getting back with Megs in January, so I said, 'Thank you, Miss.' Like I really meant it.

Then she gave me what I guess was supposed to be a smile, but it looked more like a snake unhinging its jaw.

I had a little think on the way back to class and promised myself that I would not get into any stupid scrapes next term. That doesn't mean that I can't hope that Ramsbottom will get herself into one though.

It was the choir's last rehearsal tonight before the concert on Tuesday. I popped along to Juicy Lucy's with everyone afterwards, but Finn wasn't there. Westy said Ethan had gone straight home too and that it was a good job because he'd been 'a right moody pants' today.

They'd better all buck up tomorrow, I haven't got time for slackers or miseries. Tomorrow is all about me . . . ahem, I mean the dear old folk.

SATURDAY 10TH DECEMBER

Granny drove me and Megs into school to pick up the boxes. Once again I tried to tell Granny that she really wasn't required, but she pointed out that the old people's home were unlikely to let in a horde of youths without her to explain who we were.

Being in a car with Granny is a bit like being in a cell with a psychopath. You mustn't say anything to excite her. If the conversation gets more interesting than the weather she is completely distracted and then she takes her eyes off the road and next thing you know you've crashed into a traffic light.

Today was a fairly smooth journey, Megs did a great job of keeping things calm by telling an extremely long and boring story about shopping for her mum's Christmas present. The only sketchy moment was when Granny spotted a woman wearing the hat she's been thinking about buying. We did briefly mount the pavement, just so that Granny could get a closer look. I whispered to Megs, 'My car skills don't look so bad now, do they?'

She said, 'Actually I was just thinking that now I know where you inherited your driving style from.'

When we finally got to school, I said to Megs, 'Well done for making up that boring story.'

But she said, 'What boring story?' so I had to tell her that Cam was blowing her a kiss to avoid her getting shirty with me.

I was relieved to find that plenty of people had turned up. Mrs W let us into school and we picked up the boxes. Once we were ready to go we marched off to the old people's home in a long straggly crocodile with Granny at the front shouting, 'Mind the dogs' mess!' It was like being at primary school again.

I had a brilliant time. Megs and I ended up with Finn and his mate in front of us in the crocodile and Ethan, Cam and Westy behind us. Finn told me about different kinds of surfboards (I forget the details, but I can tell you that his eyes are very dark blue) and Ethan and Westy re-enacted Westy getting stuck under a desk during their History test yesterday. Good times.

When we got to the old people's home, Granny introduced us to the manager, Mrs Holden, and then we all squeezed into the residents' lounge, which was full of the oldest people I have ever seen, sat in armchairs.

It was a bit intimidating. I've discovered that old people are like cats, they will stare and stare without blushing or blinking. Granny was right at home; she was weaving between them, smiling and nodding like a princess visiting a hospital. When she got to the front of the room she started her speech. 'Now then, ladies and gentlemen, we've got a marvellous treat for you.'

An old lady with dangly earrings nearly as big as her head looked up at Granny, then leant over to her neighbour and said in a very loud whisper, 'Who's that old trout?'

Her friend whispered back in an equally loud voice, 'It's that Jean, isn't it? You know, Jean that moved in last week. You remember; her hunky grandson brought her.'

That made Granny turn a bit pink. They obviously thought that she was one of the inmates! And while Granny is extremely ancient, even I could see that she was a tiny bit younger than this lot. But Granny just did what she always does when someone says something she doesn't like: she completely ignored them and went on with what she was saying. 'These young people have brought Christmas gifts—'

'What's Jean done with her hair?' the old lady said.

Granny raised her voice, 'Christmas gifts for all of you.'

But Mrs Dangly Earrings went on 'whispering' to her friend. 'It's a funny colour, isn't it? I don't like it.'

Most of us lot and plenty of the oldies were cracking up by this point, so Granny decided to draw things to a close. 'The youngsters will be bringing tea round now. I do hope you enjoy our visit and – Merry Christmas.'

There was a bit of applause, but old people have got weak wrists so it wasn't loud enough to drown out Mrs Dangly Earrings saying, 'She's always got to be the centre of attention, that Jean, hasn't she?'

Megs and I were first to the tea urn. We filled up two cups and headed straight for the whispering old ladies. Any ancient woman who can embarrass my granny is a friend of mine.

The lady with the earrings was called Marilyn and her friend was Audrey. They were really pleased with their Christmas boxes. Marilyn said she wanted to save hers till Christmas, but Audrey dived straight in. She particularly liked the purple nail varnish that I'd put in and she asked Megs to paint her nails straight away.

'I ask Marilyn sometimes, but her hands shake too much, don't they, Maz?'

Marilyn winked at me. 'It's the gin,' she whispered.

While Audrey was telling us about the trouble she and Marilyn had caused by putting plastic beetles in the rice pudding last week, Westy came rushing over and said, 'Faith, I need that spud gun back. Bert says he's always wanted one.'

Mrs Holden popped up at our table at one point and said, 'Are these two behaving themselves? You know, they give me the right runaround, this pair. Would you believe they set the smoke alarm off last night?'

By that point I could well believe it.

'We didn't know we weren't allowed scented candles,' Audrey said contritely. But behind the manager's back Marilyn was miming smoking a cigar and I had to pretend to sneeze into Meg's scarf to disguise my laughing.

Mrs Holden tutted. 'And I don't want to be finding any more booze in your room.'

'Oh, no,' said Marilyn. 'We just like a small sherry at Christmas.'

'Hmm,' said the manager and she rushed off to stop Westy and Bert having a wheelchair race.

Audrey leant close to me. 'The thing is,' she said, 'when you get to our age, you've got to live every day like it's Christmas.' And then she and Marilyn cackled with laughter until they couldn't breathe anymore.

The old people really did seem to enjoy our visit and I was surprised by how fun it was. Bert and Westy got on like a house on fire. Last thing I heard they were arranging to meet up in the

Christmas holidays. Bert said that Westy could try some of his home-brew and Westy was promising to make some 'modifications' to Bert's wheelchair. I'd better make sure that that visit is supervised.

I've got to admit that I was quite taken aback by what a laugh Marilyn and Audrey seem to have.

I said to Megs, 'When we're old, do you think we'll be like that?'

Megs looked at Marilyn who was wolf-whistling at an old man tottering across the room. 'Look! Look!' Marilyn said under her breath to Audrey. 'Did you see him looking at me?'

But when Audrey opened her mouth to answer, Marilyn whacked her with a Christmas cracker and said, 'Shush, I'm talking.'

Megs snorted and said, 'Faith, we're already like that.'

Before we left we promised to go and visit Marilyn and Audrey again.

Audrey said, 'When you come could you bring us a few things?'

'Yes, of course,' Megs said. 'What would you like?'

'A couple of balaclavas and a crowbar.'

We're going to have to watch those two.

SUNDAY 11TH DECEMBER

I was so worn out by all my good work yesterday that I decided to spend today in the loving bosom of my family. Sam and I played a traditional Christmas game of trying to throw Quality Street chocolates through the links of the paper chain decorations. And Dad did his traditional Christmas moan about how Chocolates-Are-Actually-Quite-Hard-When-They-Hit-Him-On-The-Nose. Mum called him Scrooge and then Dad pulled her on to his lap and they did some kissing that nearly made me sick up my Hazelnut Triangle.

In the afternoon we watched *Mary Poppins*.

It was quite a nice day actually.

But you don't get something for nothing, so I've told them all to consider my company today as part of their Christmas present.

MONDAY 12TH DECEMBER

Something wonderful has happened: people are ill! I don't normally do a little dance when other people get sick (unless they are Icky Blundell, Miss Ramsbottom or anyone who has ever pushed in front of me in a queue) but these people are in the choir! A nasty outbreak of flu means that numbers are seriously down so today Mr Millet was trawling the school for last-minute replacements.

He came into our Geography lesson and said, 'What I need are musical girls with strong voices, because we've only got the dress rehearsal left, so they'll need to be able to pick things up really quickly.'

Lily shouted out, 'Crystal's got a really good voice, haven't you, Crystal?'

Mr Millet looked at Crystal. 'Are you already in the choir?'

The rest of us could barely contain a laugh. Crystal is a complete slacker. She never does anything she doesn't absolutely have to.

'No,' Crystal said.

'Would you like to be?'

'No.'

Mr Millet started purpling up, ready to tell her that he wasn't interested in her free will and all that nonsense. Crystal's blank look remained. I think she finds facial expressions a waste of energy. Mr Millet tried to squeeze his rage into something more polite. You could see it was killing him. 'Could you, do you think you could possibly reconsider, for the sake of the school. It's just the dress rehearsal tomorrow afternoon and—'

'Afternoon?' Crystal said. She doesn't like to waste words either.

'That's right. Straight after lunch and I really do think that it's your duty as a member—'

Crystal held up a finger to stop him talking, then very slowly she flicked through her contact book to look at what she had on her timetable tomorrow afternoon. 'Double Biology'. She screwed up her nose to consider which was worse. 'All right then,' she said eventually.

Mr Millet was still furious but he had to say, 'Thank you. Anyone else?'

I threw my hand up. Mr Millet squinted at me. 'You? Aren't you already in the choir?'

'Oh yes, Sir, I've been a very enthusiastic member right from the beginning, but due to a minor mis-understanding Miss Ramsbottom said I couldn't attend rehearsals. But given the circumstances and the terrible pressure that you're under with all those parents coming and since I am fully trained and very keen to—'

'Yes, yes, I'll speak to Miss Ramsbottom. Just make sure you're at the rehearsal tomorrow.'

So I am back in the choir. For now anyway. I'm not sure what Miss Ramsbottom will say when Mr Millet speaks to her, probably a big fat no. Maybe he'll forget to ask. Fingers crossed.

TUESDAY 13TH DECEMBER

At afternoon registration, Mrs Webber said, 'All the girls who are in the choir need to go down to the hall now.' I stood up, half expecting Mrs W to say that Miss Ramsbottom had told her not to let me go, but she didn't mention anything, so off I went with Lily and Angharad.

We had a great afternoon with the boys. Mr Millet did spoil things a bit by constantly interrupting to tell us what a shambles we were and that this was our last chance to get it right.

Finn was amazing. Although I think I'm an excellent member of the choir, I actually don't know much about music, but even I can tell that Finn has got a phenomenal voice. And rather nice hair.

When he spotted me across the hall he gave me a little wave, which is a good sign, but then he is quite a friendly type, which makes it hard to know whether he is *interested* in me. It's because he's so cool. I don't think I could be that cool. I'd miss skipping and shrieking.

Mr Millet had us working right up to the bell. He says we've all got to dig deep tomorrow night and really fling ourselves into it.

I shall fling myself as far as I can whilst still looking attractive.

I hope Icky flings herself off the stage.

When the rehearsal had finished Cameron asked Megs if he could walk her home. Megs managed to choke out a yes and off they went. Leaving the lonely and unloved (me) to get the bus with the loony and unhinged (Lily). I wonder what Megs and Cameron are up to?

LATER

When I got home I asked Sam if he wanted to hear a sneak preview of the treat in store for him tomorrow when he comes to the concert.

He said, 'What? You mean I've still got to go? I thought they'd kicked you out for being unbelievably tuneless.'

'No,' I said, 'I got kicked out for being unbelievably naughty, which is quite a different thing. Anyway, they've realised they can't do without me. I'm just worried that my singing voice hasn't had a lot of practice lately.'

'I'd be more worried that your squawking will ruin the melody.'

'Actually, I've got a plan to smooth over any little vocal difficulties I might have. Look at these.' I fished about in my bag and pulled out some of those reindeer antlers on a headband and popped them on my head. 'See, when people look at me in these they will be caught up in the Christmas spirit and everything will sound festive and lovely to them.' Then I gave him a blast of our first song. 'What do you think?'

Sam took his fingers out of his ears. 'I think you're going to need bigger antlers.'

LATER STILL

I'd sent ten text messages to Megs asking what happened with Cameron when she finally rang me a little while ago.

'So?' I said. 'What happened?'

'I'm not sure that it's the sort of thing that I want to discuss.'

'What? You are kidding me, aren't you? Megan, I have to listen to every single tiny detail of your life, including what you found when you flossed your teeth. You cannot be suggesting that now that you've got something interesting to say that you're not going to tell me.'

'All right, all right. Well . . . we kissed.'

'You kissed!'

'Yes.'

I can't believe that Megs has had a snog and I haven't even managed a bit of hand holding yet.

'Come on then, you can't stop there, tell me every slurpy detail.'

'It wasn't slurpy.'

'Dry then? Like when you've got a cold and you wake up in the night and your tongue is stuck to the roof of your mouth?'

'No, it was not.'

'Slimy?'

'Faith!'

'Don't shout at me! I can't help it if I have no experience of snogging. Please don't hate me.'

'Will you shut your mouth for just one minute?'

'Is that what Cameron said before he snogged you?'

Then I had to pant with laughter a bit so I thought I'd let her get a word in edgeways.

'It was nice, OK?' and I could tell even without seeing her that she was wearing a soppy face.

'Am I allowed to ask for a bit more detail?'

'We just sort of pressed our mouths together, you know, in the tradition of kissing. It was nice and gentle, but it made my lips go all tingly. Actually it made *all* of me go tingly.'

And she sounded so happy that I said, 'I'm really pleased for you, Megs. That's amazing.'

And she said, 'It'll be you next.' Which was kind and also hopefully true because surely the spirit of Christmas can spare a little tingle for me.

WEDNESDAY 14TH DECEMBER

I feel like Santa Claus must have read all those letters I wisely spent my History lessons writing, because the concert went better than I could have hoped. We had a quick warm-up with Mr Millet backstage and then it was time to get into our places. As we were filing into position I passed Finn and he whispered, 'Good luck!' And then ... he squeezed my hand! Really and truly he did. I did look down just to check that it wasn't Westy's hand pretending to be Finn's hand or anything ridiculous like that, but it was definitely lovely

Finn's lovely hand. It was a good squeeze. And I totally got tingles.

I was a bit bewildered and had to grab hold of Ethan to scramble up next to him on the bench that the back row had to stand on. Which may have caused him to wobble and grab the hair of the girl in front of him, making her squeal just as the curtain went up, but I'm sure it all looked like part of the show. I can't think why Mr Millet put me on the back row anyway. I must give off the impression of being taller than I am.

The hall was packed and the audience were all smiling (except for the brothers and sisters of people in the choir who had clearly been dragged along against their will – they spent most of the time scowling and looking at their phones). The Christmas tree lights were shining and the band were wearing Santa hats. It was all very festive. I really enjoyed the singing, it got me right into the spirit of the season, even though Mr Millet did keep glaring at me and making gestures that I couldn't understand.

When Finn sang his solo the hall went completely quiet. He's got the voice of an angel. And the hair too. When he hit the long note I made a silent wish that I could find him in my Christmas stocking. Then Ethan elbowed me in the ribs and whispered, 'Third row back, second from the left.'

And when I looked at that spot in the audience, there was Mr Hampton picking his nose. I had to bite my lip not to laugh. But the really funny part came when it was Icky's turn to sing. She slinked her way up to the microphone to do her solo, gave what I imagine she thought was an endearing toss of her hair, opened her mouth to sing and . . . burped. Yes, *burped*.

Thank you, Santa.

She claimed afterwards that it was a hiccup, but I think we all know what we heard.

All in all it was a magical night. And now that we've got the performance bit out of the way we've got the main event to look forward to: the choir party on Saturday. I hope Finn takes the opportunity to do a bit more hand squeezing. I wonder what I should wear. I was thinking of trimming a miniskirt with tinsel.

THURSDAY 15TH DECEMBER

This morning we nipped into the corner shop near school to buy a little something to see me through till breaktime. I'd just picked up a packet of Monster Munch and a couple of Milky Ways when guess who we bumped into? Finn. Actually, it was Megs who almost bumped into him, but I selflessly threw myself between them to prevent any injuries.

Finn said, 'Hi, Faith, I'm just maxing my energy levels.' He held up a banana and a cereal bar.

'Me too.' I ditched my snacks and grabbed the nearest piece of fruit, which happened to be a rather ancient-looking pineapple.

He said, 'Cool.' And then we all stared at my pineapple. 'I'm just going to pay.'

Like an idiot I followed him to the till with my withered pineapple. Let me tell you, exotic fruit is expensive; it's just another reason to eat chocolate. But it was worth it because when we got out the door Finn said, 'Are you coming to the choir party this weekend?' Which sounded to me like he wants me to be there.

'Yes. Definitely.'

'Excellent. I'll see you there.'

Even Megs had to admit that it seems like he is completely in love me. (Actually, she said, 'He is quite friendly to you.' But, same difference.)

I can't wait for Saturday.

The rest of the day was the usual end-of-term fun. In our tutor group session, Mrs Webber put on a video for us and then settled down to write her Christmas cards. After that we had a whole school assembly. I had just got myself comfortably positioned for a snooze with Angharad as a pillow when she started doing her squirrel impression and pointing at Miss Pee like she was a particularly big nut (which of course she is). I took my fingers out of my ears and had a little listen. Miss Pee was introducing a lady from Enabling the Elderly. The lady moved to the front of the stage.

'I'm here to congratulate all of you for the hard work you have put into supporting our Christmas box scheme. It is so refreshing for us to see young women taking an interest in others and giving up their time to do good. I would like to single out the young lady who organised your contribution for praise. Faith Ashby, please can you come up here?'

Well. By Rudolph's red nose, I was not expecting that. So up I hopped and collected a delightful certificate and (more interestingly) a large box of chocolates. Miss Pee seemed rather confused to see me being congratulated and I'm sure I saw Miss Ramsbottom retching. Brilliant. There was a storm of clapping and my row were on their feet. Lily even risked a little, 'Woo!'

Best of all, as I was handing out chocs to my mates after school, Icky sauntered past to have a good gawp.

I said, 'I would offer you one, Vicky, but I know that you're allergic to dairy products.'

'What do you mean? I'm not allergic to dairy.'

'Oh. Sorry. I just assumed. I couldn't think of any other reason why you always smell like sicked-up milk.'

It seems I am both kind to old folk and hilarious.

LATER

Sam has ruined my chocolaty day of triumph. For some reason when I was giving him a sneak preview of the choir concert he recorded me and now he is using my singing as his ringtone. Ordinarily, this might not have been a big problem, but clearly I had a sore throat starting when I gave him that performance because, unlike my usual striking tones it sounds pretty bad. Terrible in fact. And now he is threatening to use the recording in other ways.

I must get that phone.

FRIDAY 16TH DECEMBER

School finished at lunchtime and it should be all merriness and mistletoe, but there is a slight problem. When I got home I saw Sam texting, so I took this opportunity to grab his phone and get rid of that horrible recording of me. Unfortunately, Sam doesn't recognise my superior upper body strength and idiotically attempted to put up a fight. While we were struggling on the floor he crashed into the Christmas tree and knocked it over. At that exact moment Dad walked in the door. Now we're both grounded. And Dad is saying that this means I can't go to the choir party tomorrow. Having wasted his own youth doing his homework and polishing his shoes, he is determined to spoil mine. I'm going to have to try to talk Mum round.

SATURDAY 17TH DECEMBER

This morning Mum barged right into my room. I was trying to sleep, but old patchouli pants rudely interrupted.

'Faith, I try to make this house a haven of calm and order. Is there any chance all these cups and plates are going to make it downstairs before Christmas? Or shall I just trim them with holly now?'

My parents keep on thinking they're funny. I have spoken to them about this. Sometimes I think they don't listen to a word I say.

I moaned. 'Ah!' I clutched my face. 'My eyes, my beautiful eyes!'

Mum bent over and said, 'Faith! What is it? Have you hurt yourself? Let me see.'

'Oohh, oww! It's ... It's your wit. You have blinded me with it.'

Mum snapped upright. 'That's not funny.'

'That's where you're wrong. I had the same conversation with Mrs Mac in Biology last week. I had just demonstrated how much more realistic the skeleton looks with pickled onions for eyes when she asked me if I thought I was amusing. I said, "Look around you, Mrs Mac; twenty-eight Year Tens wetting themselves can't be wrong".'

Mum puffed out her breath. 'I can only hope that you're embroidering on that story for my benefit and that you weren't actually that breath-takingly rude to one of your teachers.'

I patted her arm (quite kindly, because she is one of those unnecessarily hysterical types), 'One should always have hope, Mum.'

Mum narrowed her eyes.

'I know that I try to keep up the hope in my bleak and blighted existence . . .' I fixed my eyes on the mid-distance and put on a rehearsed expression of gentle goodness under the strain of uncalled-for pain and punishment.

Mum just started stacking the scattered plates on my floor and ignoring me in quite a childish way.

I wiped a hand across my forehead and said, 'Do I look pale? I think I might be suffering from that thing you get when you don't get enough sunlight.'

'Is this about being grounded?'

'Or my house arrest, as I described it to Childline.'

'Faith, you and your brother have been warned

about fighting. I don't know why you two can't have a more harmonious relationship.'

'Because he is a toad.'

LATER

So now I am trying to cheer myself up with some loud music and by trying a different style of eye makeup on each eye, but suddenly it all seems pointless. Why am I bothering when there are deprived children in the world with nothing to look forward to this Christmas? No love or light in their lives. I know exactly how they feel. It is a sad time when glitter eyeliner in peacock-blue can do nothing to raise your spirits.

But I can't sit around here feeling terrible, I should not be alone and miserable. Christmas is a time for sharing; I must spread the misery. If I am fed up, they will be fed up too.

Fortunately, my grounding allows me to go as far as the shed. If I wanted to make a birdfeeder or count the things that Dad is going to fix 'next weekend' instead of having actual fun, then everything would be fine. Think I might pop down there and twist Dad's arm – I mean, see how dear old Daddy is doing.

LATER STILL

Inside the Shack of Geek, Dad was drawing on the back of an envelope. It must have been a grand plan because he was using a ruler.

I said, 'Daddy . . .'

'No.'

'But—'

'No.'

'Weshouldpaintthekitchen.'

'N— What?'

'Mum would be so happy, she has been asking you quite patiently and with only a little bit of whining for months. Imagine how pleased she would be and how impressed your elderly, I mean lovely, friends would be when they come to visit. "This is a man who uses a ruler when he draws up plans," they would say.'

'It's a big job, Faith. Maybe next weekend.'

'I could help you.'

He made a gaspy noise.

So I said, 'I'm really good at painting; my Art teacher says my work is unbound by conventions of style, coordination or taste.'

I left him with that thought. But the day is ticking on. The party will be starting in a couple of hours. It's time for action.

LATER AGAIN

The thing about doing anything around the house is that it is not as complicated as parents make out. The main thing is just to get cracking. For example: doing the washing. There is no need to poke all of Dad's socks out from under the bed. If the little stinkers have returned to their natural habitat, leave them there, I say. Also, no faffing about sorting things into colour piles; we all know that scientists have invented the mobile phone, the iPod and lash extension mascara – surely we can trust them with our knick-knocks? This is why I can have the washing on and be watching TV in five minutes whereas Mum takes half an hour 'doing it properly'.

It's the same with decorating. Best just to get going. Obviously I am not a complete pillow, so I moved a few manky pans and things to one side before I started to slap on the lavender paint. By the time Dad made his way from the shed with all his equipment (including two rulers and an extendable tape measure – this must be a big job) I had covered most of the wall above the cooker.

Dad turned pale and launched into mega rant, 'Faith! . . . Dust sheets? Priming the surface? Undercoat? This . . . this isn't the way to decorate . . . You've got to . . .'

Just as I feared he'd start drawing me a diagram on the back of an envelope, Mum came in. 'My book group will be here in half an hour and— What on earth are you doing?'

Dad did some more squeaking. 'Me?'

'Dad, you are the man in charge. After all – you've got the ruler.'

Mum glared at me. 'Stop trying to be smart, Faith.'

'Aren't you always encouraging me in the pursuit of academic excellence? Now that I know that it is a waste of my precious time I shall follow my dream of dropping out of school and getting a part-time job at Topshop.'

'You wouldn't last a week working in that place.'

'Oh, Mum! The shop assistants in Topshop don't work! They try on clothes and have lengthy conversations about boys and makeup. Occasionally, they stop chatting to give dirty looks to fat people who have wandered in by mistake.'

Dad said, 'I should think you're overqualified to work there.'

Mum said, 'Enough of this – I've got visitors coming, what am I going to do?'

I said, 'Have your drunken women's group in the sitting room. Tell them your lovely baldy husband is decorating the kitchen for you for Christmas. You should probably make him promise not to sing though.'

'Yes, thank you, Faith.' Mum turned to Dad, 'That might be the best idea.' She looked around the kitchen. 'Shouldn't you have dust sheets? And have primed the surface and—'

'I'm on it.' Dad headed back to the shed.

'And you, young lady, can go to your room and do your homework.'

'What? It's the first day of the Christmas holidays. And I have got the Grump Lord of Shedville to do the kitchen – something that you haven't managed since we moved in here – and you're sending me to my room?'

Mum started thinking. I knew it was time to go for the wrinkly throat.

I said, 'Yes, of course I'll go and do my homework. I have to do a project on teenage pregnancy for PSHE. You don't mind if I pop in on your menopausal ladies' group to ask you a few questions about where babies come from, do you?'

Mum's mouth twitched. 'Clearly the only place to keep you out of trouble is a nice, safe, darkened hall with lots of scruffy-haired boys to keep you occupied.'

I allowed myself a small, but dignified squeak of hope. 'Have you seen my end-of-term report? Miss Ramsbottom did say that I'd made a real improvement, didn't she?'

'Hmm. Oh, go on then. But you must be back before eleven. And you must behave yourself over Christmas. No sulking and no polluting our happy atmosphere.'

'Of course! I'll be an angel. I'll be so good

you will feel faintly suspicious. I'll cook, I'll clean—'

Mum's face fell.

'Or not, if you don't want me to.' I skipped up the stairs.

Mum called out, 'Better hurry up; you've only got an hour and a half to decide what to wear.'

Fortunately I had laid out my dress before I'd even gone downstairs.

LATEREST

I'm ready. Waiting for Megs's dad to pick me up. Please let Finn speak to me. And maybe be a tiny bit hypnotised by my beauty. Please, oh please.

SUNDAY 18TH DECEMBER

I am so happy. You could power a string of fairy lights on the buzz that's coming off me.

Last night was amazing. When we got to school the Drama studio was looking particularly festive. Someone had dragged the artificial tree in from reception and blown up a load of balloons. Best of all they had dusted off the lighting board and dimmed the lights. Or as Megs put it, 'Ooh, snogging lighting.'

'There's no need to boast just because you're in the tongue-duelling club.' The party was an official date for Megs and Cameron. People with boyfriends are such show-offs.

We had a little chat with some of the other girls and then a little dance and then a nibble on the snacks. I like to think that I maintained my glamour and didn't dribble all over the place. At least not until I saw that they had cheese and pineapple on sticks.

Then Ethan and the boys arrived.

I heard Westy before I saw him.

'*Faaaaaaaith!*' Then he charged towards me, picked me up under one arm, and shook me about a bit. He is such a crazy banana. I am glad that we're friends again.

While Lily and Zoe showed off their sword-fighting-with-breadsticks routine Ethan came over to me.

He said, 'I hear that you've been awarded some sort of Girl of the Year prize. What was that for – hair and makeup?'

'No, my outstanding community service.'

'Oh, your granny-love. I expect you've got plans to harass orphans next term, haven't you?'

'I'd rather work with a less bite-y minority group. Like endangered tigers.'

'Speaking of snarly, scary things. It's good that you've stopped being mad at Westy.'

I blushed a bit when he said that because, thinking about it, it seemed like I had been crosser with Ethan than I ever was with Westy. Why did

I mind so much more when I thought Ethan had set me up? I looked over at Westy trying to juggle with sausage rolls.

'Well,' I said, 'it's not really his fault he's a noodle, is it?'

'You know he'd never upset you on purpose, don't you?'

'Yeah, I might have overreacted a bit to the whole thing. I don't know why, but there's something about Icky's triumphant face that makes me want to shout at people.'

'Really? It just makes me want to slap her.'

Which made me laugh a lot. Because there's nothing funnier than violence towards people I dislike.

'Faith . . .'

But he didn't finish whatever it was he was going to say because Westy came and sat on my lap and said, 'I've been very good this year, Santa, and what I would really like is Faith in a bikini.'

'Get off, you prat.'

I looked at our little gang and I was really happy. I felt like a weight had been lifted from me – and not just because Westy had got off my lap. I'm glad that Megs and Cam have sorted things out and that I'm friends with Westy and Ethan again.

I had a really good chat with Ethan. He does

make me laugh. I think I may have annoyed him at one point because I spotted Finn dancing with Icky and I got a bit distracted.

Why is Finn nice to Icky? He can't really like her. It must just be because he's such a sweet friendly person that he's nice to everyone.

When he spotted me he came over and said, 'Cool tinsel dress,' to me and, 'Good party, hey dude?' to Ethan.

Ethan just nodded and then went to help Westy pick up Cameron by his ankles. Finn smiled at me and looked at the food. 'No squeezy cheese. Hope you're not too disappointed.'

Oh dear, he remembers me spraying him with cheese spread. But I think that's a good thing really, it shows that our time together has meant something to him. It's like having a song. Except we've got a snack food. I didn't say this. In fact I hadn't said anything for a bit. I tried a smile instead.

Finn said, 'They've got pineapple. You like pineapple, don't you? You could chuck that at me instead.'

I still couldn't think of anything to say to that so I took him up on his suggestion and threw a chunk of pineapple at him.

And he threw a piece back at me. We started cracking up and I branched out and tried a handful of peanuts. Finn was coming back with a mini quiche when Mr Millet appeared and roared, 'Stop that right now! Any more monkey business and you'll be sent home. Pick that mess up.' And he stomped off to spoil someone else's fun.

Finn and I scooped up the little bits of food from the floor. Finn looked under the festive paper tablecloth that some soppy idiot (Angharad) had put on the table.

He said, 'Faith, come here. It's like a little house.' He disappeared under the table.

Obviously I followed him. Under the table I couldn't help noticing that Finn wasn't looking for pineapple chunks. He was looking at me. Then he started crawling towards me. Normally when anything crawls towards me (spiders, crabs, babies) I leap backwards, but I contained my leaping urges and waited to see what the monkey was going on here. He stopped with his face about three centimetres from mine. I really wished I hadn't eaten that sour cream and onion Pringle.

Then he kissed me!

I'd like to say that it was the most romantic moment of my life, but mostly I was thinking what a stupid position we were in for kissing. I wanted to put my arms around his neck like they say to do in magazines, but my arms were busy supporting my body weight, and then he started kissing a bit harder which made me wobble, so I shifted my right knee to get my balance. Unfortunately, I put my knee down on a chunk of pineapple and skidded so hard that I almost did the splits and hit the floor with my chin. Finn was understandably surprised by my abrupt departure mid-snog and he sat up, thwacking his head against the underside of the table.

Then Westy, who can hear the sound of head on wood at thirty paces, stuck his head under the tablecloth and said, 'Who's getting friendly under here . . .? Oh. Faith.' He didn't look very impressed. Perhaps he was hoping for Icky Blundell in a state of undress?

He did at least help me out from under the table, which was hard to do gracefully.

I could barely look at Finn, but he didn't seem too bothered by my ability to turn a kiss into a circus act. He just said, 'Do you want to dance?' So we went and had a dance with some of the others. Cameron had his arm around Megs, who nearly blinded herself by attempting to communicate with me in blinks as soon as she saw I was with Finn.

While I was dancing, in what I hope was an attractive fashion, I tried to remember the kiss. How did it go? Did I do it right?

Then Mr M told us that it was time to go and that there were a lot of parents waiting in cars outside. I was devastated. I was convinced that I'd ruined my only snog opportunity this year, but when we went to get our coats Finn said, 'Come here, Faith, give me your number.' So I did and then he rang my phone so that I would have his number (his *real* true number, now no one can fake me out). I was fumbling to put my phone away when he pulled me down a dark corridor. This time there was no cocktail fruit to cope with and . . . it was amazing. Quite soft to start with and then a bit more intense. I wasn't really thinking any of this at the time though because I could hear that singing in my head again.

Afterwards, I felt quite faint and I started to think that there was something to be said about kissing on your hands and knees. It would be easier to have a little lie-down when you start feeling light-headed.

Then Finn kissed me again and said, 'Merry Christmas, Faith.' And off he went.

So I've actually had my first kiss and the second one too. In fact, I'm probably up to about number seven. I wonder how soon he will ring me. He will ring me, won't he?

LATER

If he doesn't ring me it's OK because Ryan from the football team is having a New Year party and I'm sure Finn will be there.

LATER STILL

I've been thinking. The reason I know about Ryan's party is because Ethan mentioned it last night. The thing is, I wasn't exactly giving him my full attention when he told me about it because it was when I was watching Finn dance with Icky. Ethan said something about Ryan having another party and asked me if I wanted to go. And I said, 'Yeah, sure.' Because at the time I thought that he meant, 'Ryan's having a party – let's all go.' But now ... Now, I am wondering if he meant it in more of an invitationy way. Like a date. Have I accepted a date with Ethan? Wouldn't that be wrong when I've been kissing Finn? Obviously, it's Finn that I really like. He's the one I want to go on dates with.

So, why has my stomach filled with bubbles at the thought of a date with Ethan?

I need to calm down. Just because I have agreed to see my *friend* at a party it doesn't make me a two-timing Granny-wannabe. Besides, it's not like Finn has asked me to the party too.

LATER AGAIN

I've just got a text from Finn asking me to Ryan's party.

It's going to be an interesting New Year.